The Caretakers

By Robert T. Dodd

This story honors two camps in New York's Harriman Park and the men and women – the caretakers – who have run and maintained them. One, Ma-He-Tu, serves girls from the New York metropolitan area and has done so for more than 75 years. The other, Camp Trexler, closed three decades ago but still glows in the memories of hundreds of boys, the author included, who now have children and grandchildren of their own. Alumni of Camp Trexler will find many familiar scenes in this novella. Others who remember summer camps fondly should also enjoy spending a few months with Ron and Jan Tyler on the fictional Lake Menomini.

I thank my wife, Marya, for patience with my distraction while I wrote *The Caretakers.* I am grateful to her, Regina Colangelo, Laurine Marlow, Garet Church, Pat Del Grande, Pauline Royal, and Catherine Kaputa for reading the book as it developed and suggesting ways to improve it.

Robert T. Dodd

Table of Contents

4

.

1, The Wide, Straight Road

On a Sunday morning In early January, 2010, bronzed by a post-Christmas honeymoon in Naples, Florida ("budget hotel, million dollar beach"), Ron and Jan Tyler were seated at the kitchen table in their new apartment. Jan was browsing through want ads in *The North Fork Herald,* hunting for a dresser and chairs to fill their nearly empty flat. Ron was scanning "Automotive, Used," hoping to find a replacement for his 1990 Civic hatchback, which was hinting that 20 years of faithful service was enough.

"Nothing!" he growled. "They're all too pricey, scary, or both!" Frustrated, he turned idly to "Help Wanted" where a boxed ad caught his eye: "Lake Foreman, Mill Run State Park. Temporary position (up to one year), minimum wage plus housing. Call…"

"That's odd," he said.

"What?"

"Mill Run Park is hiring. Just two years ago, the state laid off a third of its staff and closed five small lakes."

"I remember that," Jan said. "Business people, my Mom and uncles among them, thought it was a good way to save money during the recession."

"I know," Ron said. "I was on the other side!" He loved the park. He had camped there for three summers and had worked for three more before a drowning forced his camp to close. He had tiptoed around Jan's conservative mother but had marched the campus with other students carrying a sign: "Save the Mill Run 75." He had marched again, with a black armband, when the bill to fire park staff passed in the legislature and was signed by Governor Simkins.

"The vote was close," he said, "and could have gone the other way. The workers had a lot of support from public employee unions and upstate legislators led by Gus Schneider." He chuckled.

"What's funny?"

"I'm picturing old Gus, a rich pig farmer/legislator from New Westphal, railing at the senators in a wild mixture of English and German. It made the papers all over the state!"

"Obviously yelling didn't work," Jan said.

"Nope. At the last minute, an environmental group with a big following on the internet lobbied for the layoffs and closures. They tipped the balance."

Jan stood up, went to the refrigerator, and pulled out hard boiled eggs, mayonnaise, and lettuce. "Why would greenies want to close the lakes?"

"They saw a chance to return half of the park to wilderness and grabbed it."

"That's it, then?" Jan asked as she chopped the eggs.

"Yep, game over. Schneider is still fighting to roll back the layoffs, but it's wasted effort. *The Herald* used to print his rants verbatim. Now it publishes short summaries below the fold."

Ron stared out the kitchen window for a moment, remembering how Schneider had galvanized the students. He shrugged, shook his head, and sighed. "I really loved camp," he said, "but I guess it's a thing of the past, like eight track tapes and typewriters."

" Lunch!" Jan announced, bringing Ron back to the present. "It's curried egg salad, sort of an experiment!"

"I'm game if you are," he said. Jan had grown up in a mansion with two cooks. Her brother claimed she failed home economics because she burned the tea water.

Ron stood up, folded *The Herald*, launched it toward a large packing box that served the couple as a temporary wastebasket, and missed it by two feet. "You keep practicing cooking," he said. "I'll work on my foul shot!"

***

When the Tylers returned from Florida, they imagined a wide, straight road ahead. Ron was finishing a Master's degree in English literature at North Fork State University ("NoFo" to students and irreverent junior professors). He had offers of full support from both Harvard and Yale and expected to enter one or the other in the fall to work toward a Ph.D. and a career in college teaching.

Jan, two years younger than Ron at 22, had finished a B.A. in library science in December and was working part time at the university's McBee Library. She too planned to continue her education, working toward an M.A. and either high school teaching or library work.

Jan wanted "scads" of children and Ron dreamed of "enough to have my own basketball team." They envied college friends who had already started families. "Another birth announcement!" Jan groused when a small pink envelope fell out of the stack of mail that had accumulated during their week in Florida.

As alluring as parenthood was, the Tylers agreed it had to wait until Ron was settled in a job. That set badly with Jan's mother. Jennifer Edwards yearned for grandchildren to run through her seven-bedroom mansion and romp on its lawns. Frustrated by her son and his wife, who were childless after three years of marriage, she now faced a longer wait for Jan. "You shouldn't marry Ronald unless he can support you!" she had blurted when Jan announced her engagement.

"We'll support each other!" Jan had fired back. "If you think I'm going to sit home and bake cookies like June Cleaver, think again!"

There were other sore points in the couple's relations with Jennifer. She resented Ron's "dressing like the gardener" in jeans, sweatshirts, and toe-out sneakers. She called his much rusted hatchback disreputable and demanded that he park it behind the garage. When Jan pleaded for a modest wedding with just a few relatives and friends, Jennifer insisted on a 21-gun affair "in keeping with our family's position." Then, to Ron's surprise, she complained about the cost.

"She's worried about money," Jan explained. "Dad had heavy debts and, thinking he'd live forever, he had almost no life insurance. He and Mom planned to sell out in a few years, pay off what he owed, and move to a smaller house."

Jan had introduced Ron to her father, Harry, in 2006, shortly after the couple met in Professor White's Colonial Literature class. Harry, the CEO of a large chain of hardware stores with headquarters in North Fork, had begun his career as a stock boy after high school. Now the family owned an estate in Blackwater, a posh suburb in the hills east of the capital. Conservative, practical, and plain spoken, Harry was leery of "college people" and unimpressed by Ron's interest in early American poets. "Really?" he asked during a family dinner, "People get paid to study such things?"

Ron and Jan's father had little else in common, but they shared a passion for basketball. Harry, a nimble six-footer with quick hands, had played semi-pro ball for two years after high school. A limp caused by a hunting accident had ended his career, but he still enjoyed "tossing a few" at a hoop that hung from the back of the garage. To Harry's disappointment, his son leaned toward science and math and away from sports. Albert preferred computer basketball to the real thing.

Ron had played basketball for as long as he could remember. In high school, he had dreamed of playing in the NBA, but his genes had other plans. While his intramural teammates surged past six feet, he topped out at five feet nine. He managed NoFo's basketball team briefly, but had to settle for being a fan thereafter.

A fan he was. Despite their different social positions and political views, both Ron and Harry idolized the Milwaukee Bucks. With just that slender connection, they had begun to warm to each other by the summer of 2007 when a coronary took Harry out. Only after he was gone did Jan, Albert, and Ron realize how much he had done to round off Jennifer's sharp edges.

2. Storm Clouds

Jennifer Edwards was a tiny dark cloud on the Tylers' horizon in early 2010. "I can handle her," Jan assured Ron. His thesis, the book that would earn him a Master's degree, was a bigger, darker cloud.

When Ron graduated in December, 2007, Ron's advisor, Samuel White II -- "Sam Two" to students – urged him to start a Master's program in the spring term. He recommended that Ron study Francois Luquer, a New Bedford fisherman and the great granduncle of the university's revered founder, Amos Luquer. Luquer family tradition said that Francois was a gifted, though unpublished, poet.

Evidence of Luquer's life and work proved hard to find. After spending much of 2008 burrowing into libraries up and down the East Coast, Ron returned to North Fork almost empty-handed. "Press on!" the rosy-cheeked, ever positive White commanded. "Try the Library of Congress and state libraries, even newspaper archives!"

Sure he would strike gold somewhere, Ron persisted. By the summer of 2009, he was convinced that he had chased the elusive fisherman as far as he could. He still had only scraps of information to show for a lot of work, but he added some historical background, wrote a draft of his thesis and gave it to White.

"Masterful!" White exclaimed as he leafed through the draft. "Few others could do so much with this difficult subject!" Although almost every page would be peppered with his comments and cross-outs, the thesis clearly pleased him. He passed a copy to Alistair Moffett, another English professor who was Ron's second reader. Both men had to approve the thesis before Ron could receive his M.A.

What White admired as persistence, Moffett saw as wasted effort. In a note to White, he described Ron's slender thesis as "trivial, far too much about far too little!" The Englishman was known to be no fan of American poets, but Ron feared he was right. "It will take a lot of creative re-writing and at least one more round of reviews to bring White and Moffett together," he told Jan, "and time is an issue. If I don't finish my degree by June, the Harvard and Yale offers will go up in smoke."

"You should tell Professor White you're worried," Jan said.

"I should, but it's not that easy. He has done a lot for me, and the Luquer saga is important to him. I don't want to let him down."

***

Ron was reluctant to hurt White, who was nearing retirement, because they were unusually close for a student and teacher. He had come to the old man's attention in the spring of 2005, in freshman English. "How come so few poems were written in colonial America?" he had asked during a lecture on 18th Century literature.

"There may have been many more than we're aware of," White replied. "There's still much more research to do!" Ron asked so many astute questions during the course that White tagged him as promising. "Mr. Tyler," he said at the end of the term, "you should take Colonial Literature in the fall."

Flattered by the professor's interest, Ron pre-registered for his course. When he missed the first lecture, White was surprised and disappointed. When he missed the second, the professor became concerned. He looked Ron up in the student directory and called him. "We've missed you, Mr. Tyler," he said. "Is there a problem?"

"I just can't go on," Ron said, his voice muted and listless. He explained that a drowning had forced him to leave his camp job in July. He was still reeling a month later when a young woman from an elder tour company called him with even worse news. "One of their buses had hit a moose near Yellowstone and flipped over," Ron told

White. "Seven people were killed, 14 injured." He stopped for a moment, trying not to sob. "My mother died at the scene. Don, my father, died the next day in Jackson Hole's St. John's Medical Center."

The only child of two ageing schoolteachers, Ron had only two close relatives, a great aunt in a Seattle nursing home and a third cousin in Los Angeles whom his father had described as "distant, in two senses." Crushed by grief and facing a mountain of paperwork, he had collapsed. "I just can't go on!" he repeated.

"You must!" said White, gently but firmly. "My lawyer will help you with the paperwork. Come to my office tomorrow morning. We can discuss what to do about your school work."

"But your course…?"

"Drop it! You can take it next fall."

White helped Ron trim his fall schedule and took him on for a course of directed reading that brought the two men together for an hour each week. By finding him things to do in the English department – tutoring, editing, library research – he kept the grieving student too busy to yield to depression.

By September of 2006, Ron was almost himself -- "light grey" as he put it. Then, when he took his seat for the first meeting of Colonial Literature, a blue eyed, curly haired blonde at the next desk leaned over and whispered, "Hi, I'm Janice Ann Edwards. You?"

Sam White had almost literally saved Ron's life. Jan Edwards would complete the therapy that the old professor had begun.

***

Neither of Ron's problems was on the newlyweds' minds as they settled into their apartment, but more dark clouds were gathering. When he visited his departmental mail slot two days after they returned from Florida, Ron found a memo from the English chairman: "Because of a cut in the university's budget, all teaching assistants will go on half salary for the spring term." He went on to explain, apologetically, that "support cannot be guaranteed for the summer either."

It was a blow. Ron had hoped to replace his wheezy old Civic, but that was out of the question now. On the bright side, he had a tiny inheritance from his parents and was sure he could pick up a few dollars tutoring in English or in German, his college minor.

While Ron was weighing whether to tell Jan about the chairman's memo, she burst into the apartment, three hours earlier than expected. Her blue eyes were red-rimmed. Her jaw quivered. "Damn them!" she exclaimed, throwing her purse on the floor. "*Damn them!* No warning, no discussion, just a note: 'We're sorry, Ms. Tyler, but circumstances beyond our control force us to reduce our part-time staff.'" The library too had felt the legislature's axe.

Ron wrapped his arms around her. Almost a head shorter than he, she seemed even tinier now. He tousled the curly blond hair that had caught his eye in White's class. "We'll get by." he whispered, but he couldn't see how. His inheritance would carry them for only a month or two. Even if he put off repaying his college loans, there was no way to make up for the loss of half of his salary and all of hers. They had to earn enough between them to squeak by until they moved to Cambridge or New Haven in the fall.

The road ahead had seemed wide and straight under the Florida sun. Now it looked narrow, winding, and uncertain.

***

In a normal January, there would have been enough turn over between semesters to pry open the job market at the university. In 2010, recession-driven cutbacks stranded many others beside the

Tylers. They spent five days poring over bulletin boards across the campus and reading every newspaper and penny saver they could find but found nothing. "Help wanted" ads came and went like summer lightning.

They were almost desperate enough to ask Jan's mother to take them in when Ron remembered the ad in *The Herald.* One morning while Jan was out revisiting bulletin boards, he retrieved the newspaper from the trash box and reread the park's ad. *How much time would it take,* he wondered, *to supervise an abandoned lake? If housing is provided, might "min. wage" be enough for us to live on for a few months?* He picked up his cell phone, dialed the number in the ad, and found himself speaking to Jack McManus, the park's Assistant Superintendent.

McManus said the lake mentioned in the ad was Menomini, which Ron remembered as the westernmost and smallest of the park's seven lakes. "It's officially closed, but we need someone to watch for fires and roust trespassers." When Ron asked whether the foreman's cabin was modernized, McManus laughed "It's probably more up to date than your apartment in North Fork!" He explained that shortly before the recession, the state had upgraded the park's communications – cell service, wi-fi, DSL – and added inside plumbing to its ranger cabins and nature museums.

Jan would appreciate the modern plumbing, but Ron was more interested in the park's communications. With his laptop and internet service, he could work almost as well on Menomini as in North Fork. If he needed something from McBee Library, North Fork was just a short drive away.

"I'm an old camp hand," Ron told McManus, "three years as a camper and three on staff, and I really need a job to carry us till fall." Realizing that the ad in *The Herald* was more than a week old, he added, "I guess there are other applicants."

McManus laughed. "Yours is the first call! I guess 'temporary' and 'minimum wage' scare people off. That and the idea of living in the woods!" Ron said he'd send a copy of his resume' and thanked him for his time. McManus said he'd be in touch if other people applied, but Ron had a feeling the job was his if he – they -- wanted it.

When Jan came home in the late afternoon, she was sullen. "Nothing!" she growled and threw her coat on a chair. Seeing that she was in no mood to hear that he wanted to move them to the mountains, Ron mixed a shaker of sours, turned on the oven, and took out a frozen pizza. He was pleased to see that the freezer also contained a half gallon of butter pecan, Jan's favorite ice cream.

"You want us to go where?" Jan asked when Ron told her about his conversation with McManus. Unlike him, she had had no camping experience. Harry sent her to Bilberry Notch, an upscale Vermont camp, for two weeks when she was twelve. Her stay ended after three days with a tearful call to Jennifer. Harry didn't repeat the experiment.

"It's just to hold us till we move to Cambridge or New Haven," Ron said, "eight, nine months at most."

"Can I at least see the cabin before we decide?"

"Sure. It's just a two or three hour drive. Let's go this weekend."

Ron called the park again. "I'll meet you there at – say – 11 a.m. on Friday," McManus said. "We're knee deep in snow now, but the roads should be clear by then."

3. Mill Run

Mill Run State Park lies just east of, and is named for, a stream that rises north of New Westphal, the state's second city and flows south to North Fork, the much bigger state capital (pop. 134,000). The stream is narrow enough to leap across in semi-rural New Westphal, where corn is king and some pig farmers are wealthier than most North Fork bankers. As it meanders down its broad valley past farms and old mill towns, it takes on water from Abenaki Brook and many smaller tributaries. Broad and deep enough below Purlin for small boats to navigate, it swells to almost a quarter mile wide just above the capital. There, it joins the Mississippi-bound river for which North Fork was named.

Historians tell us Native Americans and French-Canadian *voyageurs* used Mill Run often, portaging around rapids and waterfalls that would one day power paper and textile mills. Today, kayakers paddle the river's tranquil stretches while more intrepid souls bounce over its riffles and tumble down its smaller falls on rubber tubes.

A modern traveler who wants to go between New Westphal and the capital has several choices. A subsidiary of United offers limited, and expensive, plane service between North Fork International and New Westphal's Hancock Field, a converted Air Force base. Amtrak, slightly cheaper, runs passenger trains twice daily on the modernized tracks of the old North Fork and Mineville Railroad.

Someone on a tight budget can drive between the cities on one of two highways, both numbered 15. Old Route 15, now 15A, lies west of Mill Run. The two-lane, blacktop road's condition varies from good to fair by county and with the season. Passing through towns that call it Main Street, it winds through forests and past dairy farms, with the river often in sight. Just above North Fork, it crosses a suspension bridge over Mill Run. From there, it runs south through the capital's eastern suburbs, ending at the university.

A trip on 15a is delightful, its pleasures including stunning views of North Fork from the east side of the capital's namesake river. It is also long: Leave North Fork after breakfast and, hay wagons and commuter traffic permitting, you will reach New Westphal just in time for dinner.

Drivers in a hurry, the Tylers included, can take the faster Route 15 up the valley. A four-lane freeway completed in 2006, it lies east of Mill Run, avoiding all towns and most farm traffic. A driver who obeys its 65 m.p.h. speed limit can cover its 275 miles in about four hours.

***

"Best we leave early," Ron told Jan on the Thursday night before their appointment with McManus. "There's likely to be heavy commuter traffic on the bridge and it'll take us 15 minutes just to get through the university to 15A!"

The Tylers' apartment is in huge block of housing that the university carved out of farm land in 2004 to accommodate a quarter of its 20,000 students. Located at the south end of the sprawling campus, the complex is inconvenient for all of the university's students but those in the adjacent College of Agriculture. Ron calls it, wryly, "equal opportunity housing:"

They couple was on the road by 7:30 a.m. on Friday. Shortly after they reached Route 15A, the southern outskirts of North Fork appeared on their left. "There's Capital Mall," Ron said, pointing across the river at a half dozen stark concrete towers that all but eclipse the majestic, 1912 capital building. "My Mom and Dad hated that mall because building it wiped out several working class ethnic neighborhoods."

Jan laughed. "My father hated it too, but for different reasons. 'Too expensive and ugly,' he said. 'It looks like a mouthful of bad teeth!'"

"Right on both counts!" Ron chuckled.

A few minutes later, the Honda passed the turnout for Jan's hometown. Near the river, Blackwatet is an upper middle class community of two story homes on generous lots. A swarm of gated, Westchester-worthy estates lies farther east. They are invisible from Route 15A, but the forested ridges on which they stand appear in the distance as an irregular gray line. "Money sure floats to the top!" Ron commented as they drove by.

"My family is only upper middle class," Jan said defensively. "No gate!"

Across the river from Blackwater, the 20th Century high rises of North Fork's business district seemed to grow out of a ground fog. The morning sun gilded the tops of buildings, the largest 52 stories high, that house the city's many banks and insurance companies. Jan pointed to one building, of medium height, that bears a huge sign: "Eternal Life." "Dad loved that!" she exclaimed. "He thought it was either a very optimistic insurance company or a mega-church."

"Was his office in that building?"

"No. It was in one of the elegant 19th Century brownstones that were abandoned when the state offices moved to Capital Mall. You can't see it from here, but it's around the corner from St. Peter's Lutheran. See the tall steeple?"

19

As Blackwater's ridges gave way northward to gently rolling land, a sign for Belfield, Ron's hometown, appeared on the right. He slowed down and turned off the highway.

"Where are you going?"

"Want to show you something. We have time."

Near the river, Belfield is a middle class community of ranches and split levels on small lots. To the east, it is rural. Small family farms, a few still prospering, alternate with fallow wheat fields whose abandoned silos and skeletal barns recall a time when the town was an agricultural hub.

Ron drove down Belfield's bustling main street. "Worked there!" he said, pointing to a Burger King. Near the end of the business district, he turned left, drove a block, and stopped in front of an imposing three story brick building with arched windows, turrets, and columns. School buses, their morning's work finished, stood in a big parking lot on one side of the school. In front, a queue of cars was delivering tardy students.

"My school, Belfield High," Ron said. "Built during the Depression."

"Your parents taught here?"

"Yes, for almost 30 years. Mom taught English, Dad math."

Jan reached over and squeezed Ron's hand. The couple sat quietly for a moment. Then he turned the Honda around and returned to 15A.

A mile north of the Belfield exit, the highway angles to the left as it approaches the suspension bridge over Mill Run. Just before the bridge, there is a turnout for the Route 15 freeway. A half mile south of that, the Tylers found themselves in the feared morning rush. As they inched forward, they looked across the river at relics of North Fork's industrial past. "This is where it earns its title as a rust belt city," Ron said. "That long, low building spawned hundreds of Sherman tanks during World War II. The other big one was a foundry, a smaller one a gun factory."

"I know about the gun factory!" Jan exclaimed. "A small pharmaceutical company bought it. My brother worked there for a year before he joined a bigger firm near the university. *The Herald* says a Japanese producer of big screen TV's has bought the tank factory. So there's hope for a revival!"

Ron shook his head. "Maybe a little one, but the high tech firms that are springing up around the university are a much better bet for North Fork's future."

After a ten minute delay, the Civic turned onto the northbound freeway. "This will be a new experience for me," Jan said.

"You've never been up Mill Run?"

"Only as far as Purlin. Mom and Dad took us kids there for an art show. Albert was ten and I was eight. All I remember about it is that the trip up took forever!"

Ron laughed. "At least two hours! Your father was probably stuck behind hay wagons on old 15 and jolted by not quite level crossings on the old North Fork and Mineville Railroad." He pointed across the river at a sleek northbound passenger train. "It's Amtrak now."

Following their route on the state map, Jan said, "I see Purlin, Boxboro, New Westphal, and the state park. Where's Mineville?"

"It's Milltown now. The name was changed in the 1880's when the town's failing iron industry was replaced by textile mills."

Driving past the Purlin exit, Ron asked, "Have you ever been to Mill Run Park?"

"Yes, but just the east side. My scout troop picnicked and swam at Seneca Lake. Albert and his college buddies skied on Mt. Garfield a few times."

Ron checked his watch. "We're a bit early. Let's take a look at Milltown. It's the closest wide spot to the cabin." He pulled off the freeway at the County Road 5 exit, turned left, crossed the bridge over Mill Run, and turned south on Main Street.

Jan wrinkled her nose. "Doesn't look like much," she said as they passed a small IGA market, a post office, and several stores, some of which bore prominent "To Let" signs.

Ron chuckled. "North Fork it's not, city girl!" Continuing south, they passed a small red sandstone municipal building surrounded by a park with a World War I battle monument. Just beyond that stood a small carpenter gothic Episcopal church of 1850's vintage. Where the town ended, replaced by dairy farms, a sprawling school complex appeared on the right. "Big!" Ron said, pointing to a dozen school buses in its parking lot. "Probably a consolidated district."

Jan's eyes were elsewhere. "Now that's more encouraging!" she exclaimed, pointing to a two story building labeled Three Towns Memorial Library. "It's not a complete wasteland!"

"Getting on to 11," Ron said. "Best we move on." He turned the Honda around in the school's parking lot, retraced their route through Milltown, and turned right on CR-5. "Just ten more miles," he said as they crossed the river and Route 15 and entered Mill Run State Park.

4. The Cabin

The stone cabin at the southwest corner of Lake Menomini was larger than Ron expected: Two bedrooms, a big living room that doubled as a kitchen and dining room, and -- as promised – a modern bathroom. "It's the biggest ranger cabin in the park," McManus explained. "The foreman was responsible for two other small lakes beside Menomini."

A fieldstone fireplace promised plenty of heat for the cabin's common room, but small electric heaters in the bedrooms suggested that more was needed during the winter. Curious, Ron turned on a heater and wasn't surprised to see the lights dim. If he and Jan lived there, they would have to make do without the microwave that they used for most of their meals at the university.

"It's crummy!" Jan whispered as she pictured her grandmother's Limoges china on rickety shelves and the family silver in a drawer that had recently housed mice. "And I thought the hotel in Naples was bad!"

"It's bigger than our flat at the university," Ron said, "and it's not forever." Because Jan's frown and downturned lips showed she was not convinced, he played his ace. "Of course, we could just crash with your mother till September. She'd love that!"

Jan scowled, but his point was unassailable. She had often been crosswise with Jennifer, never more so than when she married below what her mother regarded as her station. She would sleep in a teepee on NoFo's football field before she'd move in with Mom. "Okay," she sighed.

"We'll take it!" Ron said to McManus, forgetting that he had not yet been hired.

McManus laughed. "You're still the only applicant, so the job's yours! Plan to start in early March: You'd be fighting with snow before then!"

As the Tylers stepped out of the cabin, Ron pointed to its detached garage. "What's in there?"

"Mostly junk: A tractor, a sometimes works mower, some garden equipment, and…"

Jan's ears pricked up. "Garden equipment?"

McManus nodded. "Mary Steele, the last ranger's wife, cleared a little patch by the front door and planted a few flowers." He scraped snow away from behind a row of rocks that framed the garden and pointed to a few green tips. "See? Her daffodils are starting to show because of our warm December. Don't know if her lilies made it through."

Lilies! Jan thought. Tears formed at the corners of her eyes as she pictured her father's cherished lily bed. She brushed them away.

"If you're interested," McManus said, "there's an Agway garden shop in Purlin, the next town south of Milltown."

"Great, Ron said. "We'll check it out in the spring."

***

Ron was bubbling as he drove the Civic out of the park on CR-5. "There's an old Hebrew proverb," he said. "'Whenever God shuts a door, he opens a window.' We're still on track for Yale or Harvard, with just a short detour in a beautiful part of the world!"

Jan was not impressed by either Ron's proverb or the ranger cabin. She scowled, stared straight ahead, and said nothing. *She'll come around*, he thought as they turned south on the freeway. *She may even enjoy the woods once she gets used to them.*

The Honda hiccupped before it settled into a purr on Route 15. "Hear something?" Ron asked

"What?'

"Sounded like someone chuckling."

"Probably one more thing that's about to let go!" Jan growled.

Was the sound from a balky valve? A failing strut? Or was it a hint that the Tylers would soon learn about another old proverb more relevant to their situation than Ron's? "Men plan," it says, "and God laughs."

5. Menomini

In late February, Ron drove to Mill Run Park's administration building on Lake Seneca to get the keys to the ranger cabin and find out what was expected of him. Jack McManus wasn't there. His boss, Will Orville, welcomed Ron, offered coffee, and said, "Jack tells me you're an old hand in the park."

"I camped and worked on Lake Abenaki from age twelve to 18."

"At the Y camp?" Orville asked.

"There at first, then at Camp Luther, until…"

Orville frowned. "Until it closed?"

Ron nodded. Reluctant to talk about Luther, he changed the subject. "What can you tell me about Lake Menomini?"

Orville brightened. "It's quite a story! Business is light at this time of year, so I have time to tell it if you're free to hear it."

"Please," Ron said and settled back in his chair."

"Lake Menomini started out as a half mile long bog that filled a bulge in a narrow, north-trending stream valley. No one knows what Native Americans called it, but early white settlers named it Buggy Swamp. It kept that appropriate name throughout the 19th Century while a significant iron industry bloomed nearby. Scattered small mines and a smelter just south of the swamp attracted enough workers to form a village: two dozen rough cabins, two saloons, a brothel, a dance hall, and a little church."

"What kind of church?" Ron asked.

"Catholic, for the mostly Irish iron workers. The Episcopal mine owners worshiped in Mineville, now Milltown, ten miles to the west." Orville sipped his coffee, then continued.

"In the heyday of mining, the 1820's to '70's, a narrow gauge railroad brought provisions to the village and carried pig iron from its smelter to the main rail line in Mineville. That town, the biggest in the valley of Mill Run, prospered until the 1880's. Then discovery of huge iron ore deposits around Lake Superior made the small mountain mines unprofitable. One by one, they closed and the miners' village died. Weed-covered foundations, chimneys, and the skeleton of the smelter south of Lake Menomini are ghosts from the iron years."

"What became of the miners?"

"Many found jobs in textile mills that had sprung up at riffles and falls along Mill Run. Their sons and grandsons did well in that industry till the late 1920's, when it too withered and died."

Orville excused himself to take a phone call in the next room. While he was away, Ron walked over to a large, wall-mounted relief map. It reminded him that the eastern and western halves of the park are very different. To the east, two large lakes are nestled among domical mountains, many of them more than 2000 feet high. The highest, Mt. Garfield, reaches 2850 feet and has several ski slopes.

The western half of the park is lower and much less dramatic. Its five lakes, none more than two miles long and a half mile across, lie between north-trending ridges few of which top 1000 feet.

"Admiring the scenery?" Orville asked when he returned.

"Yes. Let me guess that the bedrock differs from east to west."

"Right you are! Granite domes on the east, various folded metamorphic rocks on the west. That's where the iron deposits are."

Ron returned to his seat. Orville continued his history.

"In the early 1930's, Buggy Swamp and the ridges between it and Milltown were swept into the new state park. Creeks and bogs dotted the area because of its glacial history, but bodies of water were few and small. To make room for campsites and other recreational facilities, the state had to dam streams and create lakes. The Civilian Conservation Corps built an earthen dam across the north end of Buggy Swamp, converting it to a small pond. They christened it Little Bear, reasoning that no one would want to camp beside, or swim in, Buggy Pond. Then they built the first two of five camps that would eventually ring Lake Menomini. Two years later, they added a stone ranger cabin that stands near the southwest corner of the lake."

"Our cabin?" Orville nodded.

"Early in the Depression, the state reevaluated Little Bear Pond. It was so shallow that lilies and cattails were overrunning swimming areas that were just a few years old. To deepen it and make room for more camps, the Corps of Engineers built a higher concrete dam a half mile north of Little Bear, in a narrower part of its stream valley. This added a north-pointing pinkie to the fist-shaped pond and widened it a bit. The Park Department named the enlarged pond Little Finger Lake.

"In 1937, an Indian-obsessed superintendent renamed all of the park's seven lakes for Native American tribes, without much regard for ethnology or geography. Little Finger Lake became Menomini, and the CCC built three more camps along its pinkie. By the outbreak of World War II, there were five thriving group camps on the lake."

"How did they make out during the war?" Ron asked.

"Well, college age counselors were hard to come by, but all five camps survived, and they prospered in the 1950's and 60's. Then they failed, one by one, when a passion for sports and computer camps swept the country. Camp Lackawanna went first; then Theodore Herzl, a coeducational Jewish camp that stands near the old dam; and a YMCA camp on the west side of the pinkie. The last camps to go were Schoodic, for Lutheran boys from a working class area in North Fork, and Schuetzen, a German-American club camp."

Orville chuckled when he mentioned Schuetzen. When Ron looked puzzled, he explained, "It called itself a ski club, but neighbors claimed its main activities were drinking and singing!"

"Camp Schoodic closed in 2000 when its sponsors could no longer pay the rent for its site. The park gave Schuetzen a year to find other quarters then closed Lake Menomini, leaving just one ranger there for the safety of hikers and to prevent fires and vandalism. Four other small lakes in the western half of the park remained open. One, Abenaki, still had two active camps when the recession hit in 2008: Sycamore and Y-for-All."

"The layoffs closed them?" Ron asked.

Orville nodded. "The staff reductions were only intended to save the state money in hard times, but to get support from environmental activists, the legislature agreed to remove all man-made structures from the five lakes and make the western half of the park 'forever wild.'"

Orville said "forever wild" with an ironic edge that caught Ron's attention. The words hung in the air for a moment like stale smoke. Then the superintendent asked, "More coffee?"

"Thanks, no, but I could use a restroom."

When Ron returned, Orville resumed his history. "Lake Menomini was never high on anyone else's list for restoration -- too small and shallow – but it had one champion in the state Senate. August Schneider had camped at Camp Schuetzen in the sixties and had served on its board of directors. His explosive reaction to Schuetzen's closing in 2000 was reported word-for-word in the *North Fork Herald* " Orville chuckled. "It included German words that the paper wouldn't have printed had they known what they meant!"

Ron laughed too. With four years of high school and college German behind him, he had a good idea what words Schneider had used.

"Every legislative session since then, Schneider has sponsored a bill to reopen Lake Menomini. Every time, downstate legislators have howled him down. As the years passed, abandoned buildings rotted and lilies spread across swimming areas, making it less and less likely that he would succeed. Now, of course, all five of the small lakes are closed."

In less than an hour, Will Orville had taken Menomini's story from the early 1800's to the present. "What about the two big lakes to the east?" Ron asked.

Orville frowned, pushed back from his desk, and stood up. "Seneca and Mohegan were spared the layoffs, even upgraded. You see, they and the Big Moose Ski Center on Mt. Garfield are recreational. *They pay their way!*" As he had when the superintendent put a spin on "forever wild," Ron sensed that he disapproved of the changes.

Orville stood up and handed Ron a ring of keys for the ranger cabin, camps, and road gates. "I have to go to a staff meeting now," he said. "Good luck to you and your wife. Let me or Jack McManus know if you need anything"

Ron thanked him for a fascinating afternoon and left. As he walked down the granite steps of headquarters, he paused to look across the half empty employee parking lot. "Business is light at this time of year," Orville had said. Ron doubted that the lot was full at any

30

time of year: Seventy-five layoffs amounted to about a third of the park's staff, mostly service and maintenance workers.

Before he started his Civic, Ron slipped a cassette of light classics into its player and texted Jan on his cell phone. "On my way. Home by seven. Luv, Ronnie." As he turned onto CR-5 and drove west toward Milltown, he had a gut feeling that there was more to Menomini's story than Will Orville had shared with him. *Not my business*, he thought. It seemed unlikely that the park's problems would affect the Tylers during their brief detour between colleges.

He should have listened to his gut.

6. The Light

Jan and Ron had had so little time to accumulate things after their wedding that they brought little with them when they moved into the ranger cabin in early March. Jennifer had tried to push some heirloom (read decrepit) furniture on them, but they declined. They also left most of their wedding presents in the Edwards's basement: Three cocktail shakers and a green ceramic swan would be less than useful on the lake!

Moving into the cabin was easy, but Jan had trouble getting used to the quiet of the forest and the strange sounds that shattered it now and then. "Owl," Ron said when a long, low "Who-whoooo" made her roll over in bed and cling to him. From years in camp, he was familiar with most of the wild voices. If something was beyond him, he just guessed "vole" or "weasel." That usually satisfied her.

One March evening, two weeks after they moved into the cabin, Jan was drying the supper dishes and looking out the kitchen window at the lake. Ron was typing on his laptop by the hearth when she asked, "What's that down the lake?"

"That? That what?"

"A light! Come look!" Ron saved his file and walked over to the sink. Jan pointed out the window toward a camp at the north end of the lake. "See it?"

He did. "Most likely some hikers crashing at Camp Schoodic I'll go and run 'em off." He put on his parka – early spring nights are bitter in the park -- and gave Jan a reassuring peck on the cheek. "Back in a wink!"

As Ron walked down the stone steps to the road that ran around the mile-long lake, he heard Jan throw the bolt behind him. Always jittery, she now suspected she was pregnant and flinched at every creak in the old stone building's beams, every acorn that bounced off its metal roof.

Ron whistled softly as he walked up the gravel road, sweeping his flashlight back and forth to avoid frost heaves and chuck holes. Several times, a rustle in the dried leaves and blueberry bushes along the road made him freeze. It seemed too cold for rattlesnakes and copperheads to be about, but he stuck to the middle of the road to be safe. As he plodded along, he glanced across the lake now and then to see if the light was still on at Schoodic. It was and seemed to be moving near the camp's dock.

Then it disappeared. As Ron rounded the dam at the north end of the lake and headed south toward the dock, all was dark but for the faint glow of a sliver moon. "Hello!" he hailed as he walked past abandoned cabins, a leaf-littered volleyball court, and a pole with a dangling string that recalled countless games of tetherball. "Anybody there?" he called, answered only by faint echoes from up the lake.

Schoodic's dock needed work after a decade of neglect. A few nail heads had popped and some boards had rotted to the edge of collapse, but the raft that had marked "finish" for swim tests was still anchored 25 yards from the dock. Lemon lines still outlined a swimming area that was yielding to pickerel weed and water lilies.

Left in a hurry, Ron thought. At Camp Luther, Ron and the other waterfront counselors had pulled in and anchored their raft at the end of each summer. They had also retrieved the wooden lemons for someone to repaint over the winter, and weeding the swimming area was as much a rite of spring as raking leaves from under the cabins. *Put it behind you,* Ron told himself as memories of his old camp seeped into his mind. *That was then! This is now!*

He walked out on the dock, picking his way among the rotting boards, then turned, looked up the hill toward the rest of the camp, and called, "Hello!" Nothing. "*Hellooo!*" he yelled. Still no answer. He turned on his flashlight, twisted its knurled head for a focused beam, and swept it back and forth over the dark hillside. All he saw were empty cabins. All he heard was the gentle rustle of hemlocks and pines as they caught the evening breeze. *I'll have another look tomorrow*, he thought, *when it's light*. Whoever or whatever had drawn him to the abandoned camp was not about to come forward, and his tiny salary as a fill-in ranger didn't tempt him to take chances.

He stood on the dock for a few more minutes, beguiled by memories of another time in another camp, then turned to leave. As he did so, his flashlight's beam fell on something pale under the water by the swimmers' ladder. Startled, he dropped his light, which went out, plunging the dock into blackness.

Ron stood in the dark, trembling and sweating. *"Missing? Two? Oh God, no! Are you sure? Count again!"* Suddenly, the dock seemed to come alive with scurrying campers. He pictured lifeguards surface diving frantically while other counselors raced through camp, hoping -- praying! -- the boys had just left swim without checking out. Then these images were pushed aside by another: A greenish glow under the dock. As Ron swam toward it, it resolved into two young bodies, intertwined in a last, desperate embrace.

"That was then!" Tyler exclaimed, struggling to shake off memories of the tragedy and its aftermath. "An accident," the coroner had concluded. "No culpability." But when Camp Luther folded a year later after a disastrous summer, he had felt responsible. He had been on duty by the ladder that day. *Did my mind wander? Might I have seen something?* "No culpability," he muttered. "Still...."

When Ron stopped shaking, he remembered what had sent his mind on this unwelcome flight. He knelt on the edge of the dock, turned on his flashlight, and played its beam on the ladder. Most of it had weathered to a greenish black patina after decades of hard use and ten years of neglect, but the second step from the top was different. It had the gleam of fresh wood and screw heads twinkled brightly at each end. Ron shook again, but this time from excitement rather than horror. Someone had fixed the ladder recently! But who? Why? The camp buildings on Lake Menomini headed the Park Commission's list for demolition.

Ron looked up the hill again, listening for any hint of company, but heard only his own heart and the rustling trees. "So long for now!" he called, then climbed up to the road and headed for home.

When he reached the ranger cabin, Jan was already asleep. He shed his parka and boots, then stoked and fed the dwindling fire. He went to the bedroom, stripped off his jeans and shirt, and crawled into bed.

Sleep evaded him. While Jan snored lightly beside him, he tossed and turned until dawn, staring at the fire light that danced across the cabin's beamed ceiling and thinking about new wood and two small faces.

7. Milltown

The ranger job on Lake Menomini had advantages – no rent, a quiet place to write, and a few dollars for groceries – but it was ten miles from Milltown, the closest community. The Tylers drove there a few days after Ron's visit to Camp Schoodic, she to confirm her pregnancy and he to get a much needed haircut.

Milltown has seen better days. Several old mill buildings south of town and a row of company houses on the east side of Mill Run Creek, now largely vacant, recall three once vibrant companies that failed when the textile industry moved south. Some of the mill owners and managers moved with it. Descendants of others own estates in the hills west of town.

Milltown was already in decline in 2006 when the state moved Route 15 across Mill Run Creek and widened it to four lanes. Loss of the camp jobs was the *coup de grace*. By 2010, the business district, four blocks long and three blocks wide, had more "For lease" than "Open" signs. Its few surviving facilities included a tiny IGA market, one shelf in which was the community's drugstore; a pay-inside Shell station; and a Hoover era post office. The post office doubled as a bank on weekday mornings. Its ATM could be used at other times if the only teller had remembered to recharge it.

A barber shop occupied one end of what had been a thriving laundromat before camp closures took away most of its customers. Its elderly owner still kept a few machines going "for friends and a tax break."

Tessie's, an Italian bar and restaurant whose year-round Christmas tree had been a landmark on old Route 15 just north of town, was shuttered, its tree dark. After serving (some said luring) generations of counselors and older campers, it folded in 2006 when the new freeway took away most of its year-round trade.

"The town seems to be dying," Ron told Jan as they parked in front of the IGA. He likened it to Lake Menomini, which was losing a decade long fight with lilies and pickerel weed. "It will soon silt up and disappear, as abandoned lakes do."

The Tylers saw more evidence of Milltown's decline when they walked up Main Street toward a big, paint-deprived Victorian house at the north end of town. Only "Moses Brown, MD" was legible on a sign in front of it. Two other names had been painted out, leaving Brown, in his own words, "not just the best medicine man in town but the onliest."

"Doc Brown is pushing 80 and has Parkinson's," Will Orville had told Ron. "Having him stitch a cut is an act of faith."

"Do you suppose he can still say yes or no to a pregnancy?" Jan asked Ron.

He laughed. "You'll soon find out!"

While Jan went to see the doctor, Ron strolled back down Main Street to the barber shop."Morning!" the lanky, grey-haired barber hailed, "You're next but two!" Ron must have looked puzzled -- there was just one small boy in the shop's single chair -- for he added, "Oh, Benny's dad just went next door for a paper." Ron pawed through a pile of magazines, most of them variations on *Field and Stream*, chose a year-old *Reader's Digest*, and sat down.

Hoss -- as Benny's father addressed the barber -- was a no-nonsense type. In less than ten minutes, the father and son were shorn and Ron was in the chair."Glasses off!" Hoss commanded. "Want it long or short?"

"Long," Ron said, slipping his glasses into his shirt pocket. Jan preferred it that way. He didn't much care.

To break an un-barber-like silence, Ron asked, "Anyone been working at the old camp at the north end of Lake Menomini?"

"What, Schoodic?" Ron nodded. "Not for ten years. Why?"

"Oh, nothing special. I'm the fill-in ranger on the lake. Saw a light down there a few nights back."

"Really!" Hoss exclaimed, taking off the cape and shaking out just a few hairs. (He took "long" literally.) "Most likely damned kids. Too much time, too little to do!"

When Ron stepped out of the barber shop, he almost tripped over Jan, who was racing down Main Street to meet him. Her dancing eyes, wide grin, and glowing cheeks told him Doc Brown had confirmed her suspicion. "November!" she crowed. "Thanksgiving!"

Ron's reaction to the news was delight with a panic chaser: It was not a great time to be on the brink of fatherhood -- broke, unemployed, and struggling to finish a Master's thesis -- but he put on a big smile and gave Jan a "bear," the family nickname for a hug.

***

On the drive back to the lake, Jan was ebullient. "We'll call and tell Mom!" she exclaimed. "No, we'll drive down and tell her!" After a moment's thought, she asked, "Do you suppose the park would mind if we painted the second bedroom and bought curtains for it?"

"Pink or blue?" Ron asked absently. His mind was on his thesis, which was back with his readers in North Fork.

"Yellow, or maybe cream."

"Makes no difference anyway," Ron said brusquely. "We'll be out of there by Thanksgiving, sooner if the wrecking crew shows up to demolish the camps." He knew he had stepped on Jan's toes when she stopped talking, turned away, and stared out the side window. "I'm sorry," he said. "I'll ask Orville."

Jan was restless, eager to be doing. "I can't just sit in the house while you work!" she had told Ron when they moved to Menomini. Within a week, she had arranged to volunteer at the library twice a week and had joined an evening knitting group at the Episcopal church. She refused to think of the ranger cabin as home -- "We're just passing through!" she said when people asked her about it – but little things like the emergence of lilies in the garden and the manic laughter of loons were softening her view of it.

Pregnancy seemed to stimulate Jan's shallow Milltown roots. "Marigolds!" she exclaimed as Ron slowed down for the turn onto CR-5. "I want marigolds for my – our – garden!"

He chuckled. "Cravings already?"

"Yep!"

"McManus mentioned a garden shop in Purlin. Let's go see what they have." Ron pulled over, turned the Civic around and drove back through town. As they passed the IGA, he grunted and said, "We'd better stop here on the way back."

"What for?"

He laughed. "Butter pecan ice cream!"

8. Lower Camp

On a bright April Fool's Day, Ron awoke to find his writing blocked. Try as he would to start a sentence about Francois Luquer, his Rhode Island poet, he just couldn't. He stared at the blinking cursor for a few minutes, then crashed the computer and put on his warmup jacket. "I'm going to have another look at Schoodic," he told Jan. "Back by lunchtime."

Keeping an eye on Menomini's camps was part -- almost all -- of Ron's job as a fill-in ranger. Schoodic seemed worth particular attention. The mysterious light had not reappeared, but new wood on the dock still puzzled him. Was there any other evidence of recent attention to the abandoned camp?

The camp road, in fair condition as far down the lake as the ranger cabin, degenerated farther north into a maze of potholes, the results of a decade of unaddressed frost heaves. Ron would learn to pick his way around them in the Civic, but for now, he preferred to walk the mile to Schoodic. He followed the road around the dam, whose dry face testified to six straight droughty summers. He puffed and coughed as the road rose and entered Camp Schoodic: Years of sitting in classes and crouching over a computer had cost him the tone he had gained during six summers of swimming and hiking.

Ron recalled from the map in Orville's office that the grain of the park's ancient rocks runs north-south, as do most of its ridges and valleys. Lake Menomini lies in a narrow valley cut in soft rocks. The ridges on each side of the lake, made of harder gneiss and granite, crowd the lake, causing Schoodic and two other camps on the east side of Menomini's pinkie to have split personalities: Part of each camp lies on a narrow level strip below the camp road, the rest on a terrace some 25 feet above it. To Ron's left as he entered Schoodic, Ron noticed a winding staircase of stone slabs that led to the upper camp. To his right, a short, steep gravel road, rendered bouldery by a decade of winnowing rains, led to the lower camp and the dam.

Ron looked at his watch. Because he had promised to be home for lunch, he could spend no more than two hours exploring the camp. He decided to focus on the lower part, starting near the dam and working southward. If he had time to spare, he'd climb to the upper camp and walk it from south to north.

It was clear at a glance that the buildings in the northern part of the lower camp constitute a small village. Four log cabins of CCC vintage, improved (well, modernized) with electric lights and screens, would have housed perhaps forty boys. A tent by the water might have added a half dozen more unless a compassionate camp director realized the lakeside tent was mosquito heaven and relegated it to storage. Forty to 45 boys would have lived in what Ron christened "North Village."

Three other buildings completed the little community. One, a washhouse/latrine at the north end of camp, was of a style that Ron dubbed "neo-CCC:" The sides and rafters were made of peeled logs of 1930's vintage, but the plumbing was modern: porcelain sinks rather than the galvanized tubs that he recalled from Camp Luther; a long porcelain urinal instead of the rusty equivalent in that camp; and -- glory of glories! -- enameled wood seats over each of five potty holes. (*Imagine it,* Ron thought, *a whole summer without splinters!*) As final nods to modernity, the state had electrified the washhouse and installed shaving mirrors and outlets for electric razors.

As Ron stepped off the washhouse porch, he instinctively reached for the light switch and was startled to find that the lights had been *on.* Had the state left the power connected when it abandoned Camp Schoodic? More important, who had left the lights on? For a moment, he thought he had come upon something important. Then it occurred to him that he might have switched the lights on himself, an automatic act on entering a dark place.

Below the washhouse, in a grove of hemlocks next to the dam, stood a broad, low building with a sagging, moss-encrusted roof. Part of it was enclosed and locked. Through its grimy windows, Ron saw things –- a small kiln, some feathers and bits of fur on a bench, an unfinished lanyard hanging from a hook -- that identified it as Schoodic's arts and crafts shop.

The other half of the building, which fronted on the lake, was open but for a log railing. A ping-pong table at one end and a tattered pull-down screen at the other told Ron this was the camp's recreation hall.

Ron noticed that part of the moss-flecked floor was marked for shuffleboard, though the ups and downs of the 1930's floor boards would have made that a game of luck rather than skill. He noted too that a vigorous player might have sent his piece into the lake and -- at high water -- over the dam. Someone had spotted that problem too and had nailed down a 2 x 4 to block strays. Ron looked at the barrier carefully. It clearly post-dated the floor, but he concluded that it was weathered enough to date from the 1960's.

A flat, rectangular area just south of the recreation hall was the size of a badminton or volleyball court, with glacial boulders arranged along its sides that likely served as bleachers for spectators. The charred remains of a few logs in the middle of the court suggested it had also been used for council fires. Suddenly, Ron felt homesick. He closed his eyes and pictured pale boys, clad in face towel loin cloths, prancing and leaping around the fire while an impassive, feather-crowned chief looked on. Afraid that image might conjure up darker ones, he pushed it aside and moved on.

Beyond the badminton court stood the tetherball pole that he had seen when he first visited the camp. Past that loomed a huge handball backboard whose shredded paint and mossy boards indicated that it was abandoned long before the camp was. Noticing that one board was dangling, Ron picked up a rock and tapped it back into place, then wondered why he had done so.

One more structure completed North Village: A hipped-roof building that stood on a rocky ledge above the badminton court. Like the crafts section of the recreation hall, it was enclosed and glazed, but it was unlocked. Indeed, the door at the end that faced the camp road was ajar. Wind had scattered brown oak leaves over the building's linoleum floor.

Like the other structures in this part of Camp Schoodic, this one dated from the Depression but had been electrified thereafter. It had also been decorated: Its beaver board interior walls, painted a bilious blue-green, were covered with star charts, animal pictures, a set of 8-point antlers, and, on one of its log posts, a six-foot black snake skin. These items and the animal cages and fish tanks that crowded shelves along its walls made it obvious that this had been the camp's nature building.

About a third of the structure, the part closest to the camp road, was separated from the rest by a partition. This small room, painted the same horrid green, had been an office. A grand but long-used and much-abused, mahogany desk and an executive chair filled one corner, a pile of moldering knapsacks another. Two walls were lined with book shelves. A snake stick -- a broom handle with a rope noose at one end -- idled in a corner. Two nets (fish? butterfly?) hung from a beam.

Over the desk hung a framed topographic map on which Camp Schoodic was marked with a red push pin. Yellow pins around the red one were, Ron suspected, destinations for hikes. He opened the desk's

43

drawers but found nothing more interesting than a few paper clips and a rubber band that a decade of disuse had rendered brittle and useless. A file drawer in the desk contained a few labeled folders -- "Inventory," "Tests," etc. -- but they were empty. Evidently "Nature Boy," as Camp Luther had called his equivalent, had cleared out completely.

Or had he? On the back of the desk sat a small, gray sheet metal ashtray, crudely formed and obviously hand-made, that contained a half dozen cigarette butts. This caught Ron's attention. Why would the nature counselor clear out everything else but leave a dirty ashtray behind? Had someone been in the building after he left? Unable to do more about the butts than speculate, Ron dumped them into a wastebasket under the desk and moved along.

A glance at his watch told Ron he needed to hustle if he was to see the rest of the lower camp before lunch, but he had one more stop to make in North Village. On his way to the nature building, he had noticed something hanging by the end door of the nearest of three sleeping cabins: an arrow-shaped wooden plaque with a nested C and S (Camp Schoodic?) and the inscription "Honor Cabin." Looking down, Ron saw arcs of small rocks on each side of the cabin's steps. Anything that had grown there was long gone, but he suspected a diligent counselor had planted a few flowers. Noting that some rocks were out of place, he realigned them and stepped into the cabin.

Screens, a tight wooden floor, and electric lights had been added to the cabin since it was built, but it was otherwise much as the CCC had left it. Each end wall was lined with lockers, most of which had long since lost their doors. The side walls were half height below screens; the thoughtful CCC men had installed little shelves along them for campers' small items. A wider shelf in one corner and two adjacent lockers with intact doors told Ron that was where the cabin counselor had bunked.

Two eight inch beams that ran across the cabin caught Ron's eye for two reasons. One was that they bore black streaks next to the electric lights that hung from them, reminders of the kerosene lanterns that had once hung there.

The other oddity, a jumble of carved names and dates, reminded Ron of the petroglyphs that cliff dwellers scratched into canyon walls in the prehistoric Southwest. Many names on the beams dated from 1951; none was more recent. Ron suspected Camp Schoodic had come on hard times that summer. Hoss, the barber, would tell him later that a new, green camp director had let order break down. Older campers and staff ran wild, both groups making almost nightly runs over the mountain to town. "The trail to Tessie's was sure four-lane in '51!" Hoss observed.

Evidently, log art went out of style thereafter. Perhaps the artists ran out of empty canvas. More likely, subsequent camp directors added posting graffiti to the long list of forbidden activities that they read to boys at the start of each encampment.

Because the cabin's doors had remained closed, its floor was free of litter but for the remains of chipmunk or squirrel nests in two lockers. The last counselor had swept the place clean when camp closed, perhaps looking forward to another summer and unaware that it wouldn't come.

It was now eleven. Ron closed the cabin door, straightened the Honor Cabin sign and trotted down a gravel road that ran along the lake and linked the north and south halves of the lower camp. On the way, he passed a stone altar that stood on the shore. Its cross was gone and most of four rows of wooden seats had rotted away. Only a few stubby upright logs survived, ghosts of church services past.

Beyond the chapel, the road veered slightly to the right past the dock, then leaned left and ended below a second washhouse at the south end of the camp. Ron saw that the building was younger than the one in North Village: Rounded boards tried to simulate the CCC's log siding, but milling marks were visible even under several layers of brown paint. Frame construction, rather than post and beam; a green fiberglass clerestory; and electric lights made this washhouse as fancy as the one in North Village. It had porcelain sinks and urinals, and – Ron's purist's nose wrinkled! – fittings for a washing machine.

This washhouse was just that. Ron found toilet facilities for this part of the lower camp in a small, Depression-era outhouse that stood well above and to one side of the washhouse. One end of the latrine housed a splintery plank with three holes and, screened by a half-height partition, a rusty galvanized iron urinal. A one-hole john with an enameled wooden seat occupied the other end of the building. A close-fitting door with a hook and eye inside told Ron that the one-holer was the VIP privy and, on visiting and change days, the ladies' room.

Running late for lunch, Ron made just a brief survey of the other buildings in the southern part of the lower camp. An old-style double cabin with a central bedroom for two counselors stood just below and across the road from a large building that he identified as the mess hall.

Two other doubles stood between that cabin and the washhouse. Ron would look at them more closely later, but he assumed that the cabin closest to the road had housed the youngest kids. They would be in good field position for the privy -- important for seven-year-olds -- and under the watchful eyes of the cook staff in the mess hall. The presence of a washer connection in the washhouse now made sense, for the youngest boys were most likely to be bed wetters. Ron had dubbed this part of Camp Schoodic "South Village." Now he renamed it "Junior Village" on his evolving mental map of the camp.

He had seen most of the lower camp but had found nothing that answered his questions about who or what had drawn him to Schoodic. Then, as he started down the road toward home, he remembered something in the outhouse that had caught his eye but had seemed unimportant. He trotted back to the latrine and opened the one-holer's door. After pausing a moment for his eyes to adjust to the darkness, he peered inside. As he thought, the piece of spring steel that held half a roll of toilet paper was shiny, though such fixtures in the three-holer were appropriately rusty. When he lifted the paper and looked under it, he saw that the whole fixture was bright. So were the screws that held it in place.

Ron could barely contain himself. Trembling, he closed the privy door, climbed up to the road, and trotted around the north end of the lake, eager to tell Jan what he had found. His other clues were questionable -- he *might* have turned on the wash house lights and the cigarette butts in the nature building *might* be a decade old -- but the new toilet paper holder left no room for doubt. Someone had replaced it long after the camp closed.

***

"You found *what*?" Jan was washing the breakfast dishes when Ron burst into the cabin, panting and bubbling over with his discovery. She let the water drain out of the sink, dried her hands, and looked at him with a mixture of amusement and amazement. "You found *what*?"

"A new toilet paper holder! In the junior -- the little – latrine!"

Jan looked at him with the same puzzled frown that he had seen when he proposed to buy and assemble a knocked down Army surplus jeep. Then she sighed and asked,"Bologna or ham on your sandwich?"

Ron pulled his chair away from the kitchen table and sat down, unsure whether to say more about his discovery or drop it. He decided to drop it. "Bologna," he said, "with mayo."

***

Maybe I needed that cold shower, Ron thought that evening as he sat down at his laptop to work on his thesis. Maybe the paper holder was still bright after ten years of disuse because it had been brand new in 2000 and the privy wasn't used thereafter. Maybe there were good explanations for the other odd things he had seen as he prowled around the North and Junior Villages. *Silly*, he thought, trying to drag his attention from the camp to his poet. Junior Village! *Am I just transferring memories of one dead camp to another?*

"Is there more coffee in the pot?" he asked Jan, who was dozing over a *Redbook* in front of the fire.

"Maybe, but I'll make more," she said, yawning. She thought Ron's habit of brewing enough coffee in the morning to last the day was a threat to civilization.

"'S all right," he said. "Don't stir." Jan let torpor win out over good taste. She settled back in her chair while Ron poured a half cup of stale coffee into a small, battered pot on the stove. He rooted around for something to nibble with the coffee, found a couple of graham crackers, and returned to the table.

Luquer still eluded him, perhaps chased into hiding by his thoughts about the abandoned camp. Maybe the toilet paper holder was skimpy evidence, but what about the new board at the dock? And what about the light that had drawn him to Schoodic in the first place?

Sleep caught up with Ron before he could catch his poet. When he awoke, the kitchen clock said it was after two. The fire had dwindled to a few embers, leaving the living room chilly going on cold. Jan was in bed.

A nightmare had roused him, shaking and drenched with sweat. In it, he was paddling up a lake -- not Menomini, more like Abenaki, Camp Luther's lake. As he approached the shore, the blade of his paddle struck something. A rock? A stump? He looked down through the yellow-green water and saw a light-colored object. When he nudged it with the paddle, he realized it was too soft to be a rock. As it turned over slowly, a boy's face appeared, its eyes a wide stare, its mouth open in a silent scream.

"Just an accident," Ron mumbled as he made his way to the bedroom.

9. Bad News

On April 4, a freakish late snowfall -- no more than an inch -- decorated tree branches in Mill Run State Park as if for Christmas. Then it vanished, driven away by a warm rain that announced a week of spring-like temperatures. Ron welcomed the rain. Fire is a ranger's biggest fear after a dry winter, the more so because some volunteer firemen have been known to start a blaze, then race home and wait to be called to paid duty. Rain also kept Ron at the keyboard when he needed to concentrate on writing.

He had all but forgotten Camp Schoodic and was deep into revising a chapter of his thesis. In it, he suggested a connection between New England poetry and the cod's life cycle. The idea was a reach and might not get by Sam White ("Novelty has its place. However...") but he was writing again and even thinking about the move to Cambridge or New Haven. Jan was at ease too, her bouts of morning sickness unpleasant but oddly reassuring.

Another contributor to peace in the ranger cabin was an almost mute telephone. Few people knew the Tylers were at the lake, and the couple made most of their business and family calls on their cell phones. Indeed, the house phone was so still that Jan picked up the receiver now and then just to see whether it was still working.

Hence, the couple was startled when the phone sprang to life at 8 a.m. on a Friday morning in mid-April. The caller was Sue Ellen Baxter, Milltown's postmistress. "Package for you, Mr. Tyler," she said. "Looks like a book. Want me to hold it till Wednesday?"

"No, that's okay. We'll pick it up this afternoon." Although they usually visited their post box at mid-week when the IGA's shelves were fully stocked, Ron thought the package might be important enough for an extra trip to town.

"You go to the IGA," he said as he parked the Civic in front of the market. "I'll get the mail."

The package that Sue Ellen handed him was indeed a book: his. Ron had sent his readers draft copies of his thesis, hoping to spot problems before he wrote a final version. He wasn't worried about his advisor, who was still enthusiastic about his research on Francois Luquer. White would pick at details in the draft. He was unlikely to reject it.

Ron's second reader was another matter. London-born, Cambridge-schooled Alistair Moffett made no effort to hide his belief that Western culture would have lost little if the American colonies had drifted out to the Pacific Ocean and sunk. He held colonial poets in particularly low regard, describing the best of their work as "little better than limericks."

Nothing that Ron had turned up during his long days at a dozen libraries was likely to change Moffett's mind. Indeed his research had convinced him that Luquer gave new meaning to the expression "minor poet." "It's probably lucky," he told Jan, "that the kid wrote only two clumsy sonnets and part of a third before he tumbled off his father's trawler at age 22 and was skewered by a passing swordfish."

"What might Luquer have become?" White had asked during a lecture the previous fall, comparing the poet's truncated career to that of composer Franz Schubert. Because the question seemed to be rhetorical, no hands went up. Even Ron abstained, for he knew an objective answer, "Just an older, wiser fisherman," would wound the old man. It helped not at all that what White would condemn as heresy, Moffett would welcome as more evidence that colonial America was a literary black hole.

The package that Sue Ellen gave Ron was thicker than the one he had sent to his readers, and it was stamped "Postage due." *Not a good sign*, he thought as he counted out $2.50 for the extra postage. He imagined a forest of blue pencil marks and page after page of stick-on notes, with White urging him to "Press on" and Moffett commanding "Pack it in!"

"Is it your book?" Jan asked as she emerged from the IGA with a small bag of groceries.

"Yeah," Ron said glumly, "but from the weight of it, not just mine." He tossed the groceries and mail in the back of the Honda and handed his keys to Jan. "You'd better drive home. I just might run someone over."

***

Ron's dark feelings about his second draft were well founded. While still professed "unflagging confidence" in him, White had found enough nits to pick to keep his cursor busy for weeks. "Many of his comments suggest that he has more trouble with English than I do," Ron fumed to Jan. "I still have to answer them."

To Ron's surprise, Alistair Moffett had written just a few comments on the manuscript, most of them positive: "Bravo!" "Very well put!" "Nice touch!" However, his cover letter to White described the thesis as "a very well- played waste of time." Oddly, he had scribbled a note in the margin of Ron's copy of the letter: "Mr. Tyler: Please see me at your earliest convenience – A.M."

That morning, Ron had awakened soaring, confident that he could meet Harvard's June 15 deadline and perhaps even Yale's, June 1. He emerged from his first pass through the riddled manuscript afraid he couldn't meet either. What Professor Moffett clearly regarded as a wild goose was beginning to look like a dead duck.

10. Upper Camp

A few evenings after Ron received his manuscript, he was beavering through White's endless comments while Jan washed the supper dishes. When she was putting the silver away, she stopped and said, "I think the light's back." Ron got up and joined her at the window. He saw it too, just before it flickered and disappeared.

"Don't go!" Jan pleaded, grabbing his arm. "If he -- if it -- wanted you...." Jan had never liked a mystery, particularly one that involved Ron.

"Don't worry," he said, "I only chase ghosts in the daylight!" Jan chuckled, but without conviction.

***

Ron got up early the next morning and fixed steel cut oatmeal. He meant it as a kindness, but when Jan walked into the kitchen, he realized it wasn't. "It looks like..." she mumbled and ran to the bathroom. By the time she emerged, Ron had dumped half of the oatmeal in the garbage and had taken a box of corn flakes from the pantry cupboard. "Sorry," he said.

After breakfast, he pulled on his boots and warmup jacket and took the ranger's key ring from its hook next to the front door. "I'm going to drive around the south end of the lake for a look at Camp Herzl," he said. "Driving will give me a chance to see if the road on the east side would be passable in case of fire."

"Lunch?"

"I should be back, but save some soup for me if I'm not."

As Ron walked down the front steps, he heard the deadbolt slam. Still nervous about being alone in the woods, Jan would have been more so had she known that he hadn't talked straight about his plans. He would take a quick look at the other camps on the east side of the lake, but his target was Schoodic. Determined to find out who or what was toying with him, he hoped to find the answer in its upper camp.

***

CR-5, which passes the south end of Lake Menomini, was State 105 until someone in the Department of Transportation noticed that the narrow, winding road had more than its fair share of accidents. Rather than pay to widen or straighten it, the state palmed it off to the county. It was still one of the most lethal roads in the state: As Ron turned onto it, he noticed a small wooden cross and a faded bouquet on the right shoulder.

In the days when there was camp traffic on CR-5, the state had widened part of its shoulder to make a small parking lot that overlooked the lake. Ron imagined generations of frightened newbie campers having their first look at Menomini there. ("Two weeks? Why, Mom? *Why*?") Overgrown now, the spot offered only glimpses of the lake, but they were good enough for the many teen couples who parked there.

Ron paused at the overlook, then drove along CR-5 to the turnoff for the camps. A battered green and white sign at the intersection advertised, " M-1 Lackawanna. M-2 Theodore Herzl. M-3 Schuetzen." The sign ended with a jagged edge that cut off "M-4 Schoo...." Ron unlocked and removed a snap lock that secured an iron bar across the camp road, pushed the bar aside, and drove in, stopping to close and lock the gate behind him.

Camp Lackawanna, which had been run by a children's aid society in North Fork, stood just off CR-5, on the wide fist of Lake Menomini. It had folded a decade before the other camps and showed it. Bits of torn screen hung from windows that were more holes than glass. Without leaving his car, Ron could see that most of the buildings had shed so many boards that they were mere skeletons. Lackawanna had no future and seemed to know it. Only a few flecks of color on a forlorn totem pole recalled better times.

The camp road had fared better on the east side of Lake Menomini than on the west. Potholes were many, but most were shallow. There were frost heaves, but none that the Civic couldn't limp over or steer around. The only, but big, exception was a washout by an inlet between Camps Lackawanna and Herzl. A stream that tumbles off the ridge east of the lake had flooded the road often enough to scour out washtub-sized patches of macadam and leave deposits of coarse gravel and boulders. It would be easy to patch the road: Ron added that to his wish list for the park's road crew. For now, he'd have to proceed on foot.

Just past the washout, the road narrowed, swung sharply to the left, and wriggled through a cleft between two towering masses of granite. Barely wide enough for a car, the pass would have been a sobriety test for counselors returning from a night at Tessie's. The risk of head-on's was so obvious that someone had painted "Honk!" on a square of sheet metal that hung from a nearby tree.

Ron chuckled. *Pancho Vanilla's Gap!* he thought, recalling a similar pinch point on the road into Camp Luther. He and his college roommate had almost met eternity there when they entered the gap from opposite ends, both honking but at the same moment. Fortunately, neither was in a hurry.

Camp Herzl was bigger than Schoodic and much more elegant. Its cabins were glazed and screened; all had electric lights. A glance inside the boys' washhouse, just below the road, revealed stall showers and porcelain toilets. No doubt the girls' facilities, well above the road and accessible via a winding stone stairway, were even more elegant. Ron would take that on faith for now.

He thought it must have pained Herzl's governing board to close the camp. A new, enclosed recreation hall, its varnished log walls still gleaming, testified to a last hurrah: An attempt to spruce up the camp and stem the tide of prospective campers lured away by Camp Compute or Camp B-Ball. Clearly, it hadn't worked.

Ron poked around a few more of Herzl's buildings, less because of interest than to "do my job," then quick-stepped down the road. It was 8:30. Schoodic was still almost a half mile away.

Just past a reed-choked inlet, Ron saw a building that stood a few yards from the lake shore. Its stone walls and hipped roof identified it as a sibling of the ranger cabin. Around it stood the tattered remains of five screened cages. These and a cement and stone turtle pit that clung to one end of the building told Ron it was one of several small nature museums scattered throughout Mill Run State Park. He peered through a window in the building's massive wooden door but saw just some benches, a few stools, and, on one wall, the shredded remains of a huge Audubon bird poster.

South of the museum, a rocky path led down to a tiny point of land that extended into the inlet. On the point stood a small, square wooden cabin. Ron took this to be the nature man's (or woman's) house, and was not surprised to find, just beyond it, a circle of rocks that had held campfires. He closed his eyes and imagined the museum people sitting there on a warm summer evening, watching the sun sink behind the ridge across the lake while a pair of loons circled and ducked, circled and ducked, on Menomini's green and gold surface.

The image jolted him. *Gone!* he thought. *All gone!* Not just the boys (or girls) who introduced the mysteries of frogs and squirrels, bats and raccoons to slightly younger kids from the neighboring camps, but the way of life they represented. Camp work had been for them, and for him, a world apart from home and school: A taste of maturity -- responsibility -- in the twilight of childhood. Even more than the abandoned camps with their mossy roofs and staring windows, the museum symbolized loss.

Ron didn't know how long he stood on the point before the toot of a car horn jerked him back to the here and now. A moment later, a green Jeep four-by with a Park Commission sign on its door emerged from the gap, swung around the inlet, and screeched to a stop in front of the museum. A tall, lean young woman in a Smokey Bear hat and green park shirt popped out and hailed him. "Saw your Civic," she called. "Got car trouble?"

"Nope," Ron said, walking up the trail to meet her. "Just couldn't get it past the washout." He extended his hand. "I'm Ron Tyler, fill-in ranger for the lake."

"Edie Henner," she said, shaking his hand. "Thought you might be one of the kids who get in here to party sometimes." She chuckled. "See you're not. Take care now!"

The ranger turned toward her Jeep. Before she could climb in, Ron hailed her. "Edie, do you know... Have you seen anyone down at Camp Schoodic?"

"Schoodic?" She thought for a moment. "Coupla bums a year or two back. Lit a fire down by the lake. Otherwise, no. Why?"

"Oh, nothing," Ron said. "Just seems too nice a camp to be empty." He was not ready to share his observations and suspicions with anyone in uniform.

"It is! But my favorite spot is right there," she said, pointing toward the little cabin on the point. "My kind of place!"

"Mine too!"

Edie climbed into her four-by, revved its engine, turned around in front of the museum, and, with another toot, disappeared.

***

It was now too late for Ron to give more than a wave to Camp Schuetzen if he was to have time for a look at Schoodic's upper camp. Like Herzl, the ski club was very well preserved. A big parking area, part of which had doubled as a volleyball court, testified to a time when the camp drew people from as far away as urban North Fork and upstate, rural New Westphal.

A huge totem pole that stood by the entrance caught Ron's eye. An eagle that glowered from its top clutched a wreath, now empty, that might have held a swastika during the 1930's. Ron recalled Hoss's comment about Schuetzen that "a lot of them Müllers turned unto Millers *real* fast when W.W. II came!"

Whatever their politics were, the folks at Schuetzen had a lovely playground. A long dock and boat mooring still gleamed, only rotten in a few spots despite a decade of neglect. A huge stone dining hall, glazed at one end but open toward the lake, and a dozen electrified cabins with chinked log walls were far above the CCC's standards.

Although the camp's totem pole had caught Ron's attention first, it shared the sky over the parking lot with a tall, three-globe lamp post that would have provided enough light for night volleyball or reading North Fork's German newspaper, the *Beobachter*. Even in retirement, Schuetzen was grand enough to explain why Gus Schneider was eager to reopen the lake. Ron found himself rooting for the determined little senator.

***

The camp road curved around another tiny, creek-fed inlet between Schuetzen and Schoodic. The two camps were so close together that it was easy to imagine counselors from the boys' camp slipping over to parties at the ski club. Had the allure of Schuetzen's *Fräuleins* caused, or contributed to, the 1951 debacle recorded on the beams of Schoodic's cabins?

Ron had seen Schoodic's mess hall from the lower camp, but the view from below did it scant justice. It was huge: at least 15 by 25 yards. Its sides were open over half height log walls, but its hipped roof overhung far enough to keep out all but the most determined rain. Because the downhill side of the building might still ship water in a gale, that wall had hooks for tarpaulins. No such protection was needed on the uphill side, for the mess hall had been built into the hillside.

The building dated from the Depression, but fluorescent fixtures and a tight hardwood floor testified to a major renovation in – Ron guessed -- the 1950's or '60's. The linoleum-covered tables and some of the better preserved wooden benches were probably of similar age. Counting tables and benches, he estimated that the camp could have seated at least 150 campers and two dozen staff members comfortably, a total of perhaps 200 people in a pinch. Schoodic was a big camp.

In the mess hall, as in the camp's recreation hall and nature building, there was evidence of a quick retreat. A battered aluminum pitcher and two Melmac cups stood in the serving window under a sign that commanded, "Scrape your dishes!" More striking was a large, white window shade that hung from a beam at the front of the hall. Thinking it might be a movie screen, Ron pulled it down and was surprised to find, in bold letters: "Tireless guardian of our way, thou hast kept us well this day. While we thank thee, we request, care continued, pardon, rest."

It was an evening grace. Above it on the shade were prayers for lunch and breakfast. Ron was unsure what tune would go with the words, but they affected him in the same way as the view from the nature museum. Standing in the dark mess hall, he sensed -- felt -- a crowd of shuffling, poking kids who were more interested in who would get the choicest breakfast cereal ("Sugar Pops! I get the Sugar Pops!") than in singing. The silence hurt.

Obviously, Camp Schoodic did not just go somewhere else: Surely the staff would have taken its grace along, as Camp Luther did with its "Think of the Other Fellow" sign when the double drowning forced it to close. Schoodic didn't relocate. It just died.

Ron pushed through a Dutch door that separated the dining hall from the kitchen. Here as elsewhere in the camp, old and newer rubbed elbows. Galvanized iron sinks and a badly worn linoleum floor were either original or of World War II vintage. On the other hand, stainless steel counters, a big exhaust fan, and an upscale oven complex were both more recent additions and evidence of prosperity.

A walk-in dry closet on one side of the kitchen and a walk-in freezer on the other were all but empty, "all but" because the freezer contained two surprises. One was a five gallon tub of vanilla ice cream. Ron pried it open and found that what was left of its contents had shriveled to something that resembled white tar. Here was more evidence of a hasty departure.

The other surprise would be added to Ron's growing list of mysteries. On one of the open wood shelves in the freezer, so far back in a corner that he almost missed it in the meager light from the kitchen, was a half empty jar of spaghetti sauce. Recalling the condition of the ice cream, Ron resisted the temptation to open it, but instead looked at a string of letters and numbers that ran along its lid. Only part of it was legible, but he thought he made out "...by 12/09." *That can't be right*, he thought. He put the jar down, then picked it up

60

again and carried it into the kitchen. Standing under a skylight, he squinted at the lid and read, again, "...by 12/09."

Barely able to restrain himself, Ron returned the jar to the freezer, glanced at his watch -- "11:45" -- and scrambled down the mess hall steps to the road. Once again, he had big news to share with Jan. Someone *had* been in Camp Schoodic recently, and he (she? they?) had eaten spaghetti!

***

"Sure, it could be bums," Ron told Jan, "or kids."

"Or Chef Boy-Ar-Dee!" she said tartly. She was having a bad day: cramps, nausea, and a droopy phone call from her mother. Ron's late arrival for lunch didn't improve her mood, nor did his breathless report on the morning's news.

"What did Jennifer want?" Ron asked as he sat down to a bowl of soup.

"To bitch, mostly. 'Do you have to stay up in the woods so long?' 'Do you have enough money?' 'When will Ronald finish his little paper?' Stuff like that."

Ron grunted. He bridled at Jennifer's reference to his "little paper," but he knew Jan too was troubled by his slow progress. When he needed to focus on today and tomorrow, he was distracted by yesterday, haunted by one dead camp and beguiled by another.

"By the way," Ron said as he added Grey Poupon to a ham sandwich, "I met another ranger today, Edie Henner. Seems a nice girl."

Jan grunted. Sensing an opinion in her reaction, he dropped the subject.

61

***

The light at Camp Schoodic didn't reappear that night or for many nights thereafter, but Jan had to rouse Ron several times when his violent nightmares turned their double bed into a war zone. All he remembered of his dreams was small, pale faces. That was enough.

11. Paint

By the second week of May, it was obvious that another round of write -- review -- rewrite would take Ron past the deadline for Yale and probably Harvard's as well. He e-mailed both schools to see whether he could delay enrollment until January, 2011. Yale's response was brusque: "We regret that our offer is conditional on acceptance by June 1 and enrollment for the fall term of 2010."

Harvard, Ron's first choice, was no more helpful. "Delayed enrollment is possible in extreme circumstances," the Graduate Dean wrote, "but the June 15 deadline for acceptance of our financial offer stands." She went on to say that support for the second term and beyond was "conceivable but cannot be guaranteed."

Meanwhile, what Ron hoped was the final version of his thesis was back at the university. White would pass it through a sieve again, but he suspected Moffett would just restate his opinion that it was "a long climb for a short ski." Would he sign off on it anyway? Ron wouldn't know until he visited him in early June, painfully close to Harvard's deadline.

Dead in the water, Ron decided to take another look at Schoodic, in particular the rest of its upper camp. "I'm going over to the other side of the lake," he told Jan. "Back for lunch."

"Take your phone," Jan pleaded.

"Will do, though cell service is iffy over there."

As Maintenance had promised after Ron reported the washout near the nature museum, the road crew had filled it with gravel. It would wash again, but for now, Ron was spared a long hike to Camp Schoodic. He drove past Herzl and Schuetzen, pausing briefly at the ski club to examine two sets of tire tracks that crossed the camp's volleyball court. *Probably the road crew*, he thought, then pushed on and parked next to a small cook's cabin behind Schoodic's mess hall.

A gravel road ran north from the mess hall for a few dozen yards then widened into an almost level terrace that held the upper camp. The first thing Ron noticed on the terrace was an asphalt-topped basketball court, with an iron pole supporting a hoop at each end. The hoops were rusty, but one held vestiges of a net. On a whim, he jumped up and tugged on the net, bringing down a shower of shreds that made him sneeze explosively. *Smart!* he thought. *Very smart!*

To the left of the basketball court stood two buildings. Both had the peeled log walls and tarred roofs that Ron called "early CCC." A few logs, lighter colored than the rest, had been installed since the Thirties, but stains around rusty nails showed that the repairs were decades old.

The first building stood beside stone steps that led down to the camp road. Its moss-flecked roof covered a back porch that overlooked the road. A wooden bench in front of the cabin and other benches on the far side of the basketball court were, Ron assumed, for kibitzers.

The cabin's front door was padlocked, but Ron peered through its time-dirtied windows. He saw things -- hospital beds, shelves lined with medicine bottles, and an examining table – that identified the building as Schoodic's infirmary. A scale in one corner made him chuckle as he recalled Camp Luther's more body-proud counselors who had checked their weights after every softball game.

Rounding the corner of the infirmary to examine its porch, Ron   almost fell over a water fountain. He tried the handle and was not surprised when it yielded nothing. Next to the fountain hung an old rotary pay phone. Although its metal case was dull and pitted, the cabin's overhanging roof and a canopy of trees had protected it from further weather damage. He was about to pick up the receiver when the phone rang, shattering the stillness of the woods and sending him tumbling backward over a bench. When it rang again, he picked himself up and grabbed the receiver. "Hello?" Nothing. *"Hello?"* Again nothing, then a dial tone. He replaced the receiver and stared at the phone. *Power in the camp is still connected,* he thought, *and the phone is working.* Wondering who was paying for the utilities and why, he walked around the building to examine its porch.

The camp's nurse had had a comfortable little nest. The screened porch held a day bed, an Adirondack chair, and a small corner table with a lamp made from an antique coffee grinder. A braided rug and a framed Audubon print over the day bed completed the décor.

Recalling his experience in the washhouse, Ron tried the lamp. It didn't work, but while he was trying it, he noticed its bulb: a spiral compact fluorescent. For a moment, he relived the excitement of his earlier discoveries: *When were CFL's invented? Were they in use in 2000?* He made a note to Google CFL's when he got back to the cabin.

Looking into the infirmary's back room through a window in its locked door, Ron saw a bed, a dresser, two small scatter rugs, and more Audubon prints. He closed his eyes and tried to picture Schoodic's nurse. Was she young, blond, and pretty like Camp Luther's Nurse Betty, who had made him wish he had something wrong that she could fix? Or was she an old dreadnought like Y-for-All's Nurse Campbell, who administered a vile-smelling salve to cuts and burns and was said to give shots with a bicycle pump?

A glance at his watch told Ron he had less than an hour left before he would have to head home for lunch. He walked the few yards to the second, larger building. Like the infirmary, it was original but had been upgraded. A porch that hung over the camp road was made of rounded planks that poorly mimicked the original logs.

Fifties, he thought, recalling similar siding on the junior washhouse. By then, the park had its own saw mill.

The building's screened porch was bare but for a long table and an empty refrigerator-freezer. Its interior wall, the building's original rear, held two windows. Between them hung a cork bulletin board and a rust-flecked Coke sign of the sort that featured an elfin character with gray hair. *Forties*, Ron thought. These artifacts and the shredded remains of a price list on the wall identified the porch as the camp store. Ron concluded that the building had been Schoodic's headquarters.

He tried the door to the interior, but it and the two windows were locked. Thinking there might be another entrance, he left the porch and walked around to the front of the building. As he did, he noticed that a lattice door to its crawl space was slightly ajar. He opened it, squatted and peered inside. Although the light was poor, he made out seven carefully wrapped bales of canvas that he suspected were tents. Next to a neat stack of two-by-fours and other lumber were jars and boxes of nails and screws.

To one side, almost out of sight, Ron spotted several cans of paint, brushes, and a gallon can of turpentine. *Paint!* Ron thought. *Some of it is dated!* Stretching to reach a can, he pulled it out and carried it to a patch of sunlight between the trees. Fingers of light blue-green paint -- the same bilious color he had seen in the nature building – had run down the sides, hiding most of the can's label. Among the surviving specifications was the one he was looking for: "Lot No. 447, 11/07." The paint was just three years old!

Ron was both excited and embarrassed. It hadn't occurred to him that the paint job in the nature building might be recent. Someone had taken pains to remove posters before painting the walls and had replaced them afterward.

He returned the can of paint, restored the door to its part open state, and trotted down the gravel road toward the mess hall and his car. On the way, he glanced past the basketball court to the woods, where seven weather-beaten platforms stood among the oaks and hemlocks, waiting for the tents that he had seen under headquarters. He wasn't surprised to see that the platform closest to the basketball court had a railing whose pale 2 x 4's stood out from the rest of the structure.

He was jubilant. A search on his laptop would confirm that the nurse's CFL bulb was a blind alley – such bulbs were in use by 1995 -- but that didn't matter. He now had solid evidence that someone had worked on the camp recently, though who and why remained mysteries.

On the way back to the ranger cabin, he stopped at the overlook on CR-5 to call Edie Henner. Initially wary of the ranger, he had come to trust her enough to tell her about his earlier discoveries. He had been startled, even hurt, when she dismissed them as "just kids or bums!" When Edie didn't pick up, he left a brief message: "I think I've found the key to the Schoodic mystery. Don't call me. I'll try you again later."

Ron sat at the overlook for several minutes, staring up the lake. Should he tell Jan what he had found under the headquarters building? Upset about his slow progress on the thesis, she thought Camp Schoodic was the cause. "It's a haunt!" she had fumed when he mentioned it that morning. He was afraid suspicion about his "ranger lady" contributed to her dark feelings about the camp.

He shrugged. Not wanting to add being late for lunch to his sins, he pulled out of the overlook and headed for home.

12. Jan and Edie

Milltown's IGA is tiny and poorly stocked by suburban standards, but it has one feature that the Tylers enjoyed often: a back corner where a coffee machine, a hot plate for tea water, and a case of homemade pastries invite shoppers to linger at one of two four-seat tables. On most Wednesdays, when the prospect of full shelves brought them to town for the week's groceries, the couple ended their shopping with coffee and a Danish.

A Wednesday in late April was unusual. Their shopping nearly finished, Ron left Jan and their cart by the coffee machine and went to the refrigerated section for milk and a six pack of beer. When he returned to the coffee corner, he was startled to see Edie Henner seated across from Jan. She was wearing her ranger shirt. Her Smokey Bear hat lay on the chair beside her.

"Hi, Edie!" Ron said, settling in next to Jan. "I see you two have met."

"Hi! Jan was telling me about her garden."

"It's not much, just a few marigolds," Jan protested, "and some inherited daffodils and lilies."

"She started the marigolds herself, in peat pots," Ron said proudly. "The man in Purlin's garden shop told us they repel deer."

"I've heard that." Edie said, "A 30-30 works better!"

After a few minutes of small talk about Milltown's empty stores, Jan asked Edie, "How did you become a ranger? It seems like a…"

"Funny job for a woman?" Jan nodded and blushed.

"Well, I was a pretty good student in high school," Edie said, "but I was antsy. Had to keep moving, like a shark. I started pre-law at NoFo, thinking to go into my father's racket."

"And?"

"It was too much sitting down for me! I switched to forestry in my junior year. It was also too much butt work, so I dropped out." She paused to blow across her coffee. "Coming up on 21, I had no idea what I wanted to do. So Dad asked Will Orville, an old friend, to find me work in the park."

"As a ranger?" Ron asked.

"Not at first. In headquarters: filing, answering the phone, and such. It didn't take long for Will – Mr. Orville – to see that wasn't for me. He suggested the ranger job to 'get you the hell outdoors where you belong!' So here I am!"

Edie stood up, stretched, tossed her cup in the trash, and tucked her tightly braided auburn hair into her hat. "Nice meeting you Jan, but I should go and look busy."

After Edie left, Jan dumped the coffee cups and napkins, and the couple resumed their shopping. "Friendly girl," she said, "but she seems a bit…"

Ron chuckled. "Tough? Yes, she does. It's the Smokey hat!" Then he pushed the cart toward the freezer section and said, "Don't forget your butter pecan!"

13. The Tour

Two days later, the telephone rang while the Tylers were eating breakfast. "It's for you," Jan said, pushing the phone toward Ron. "Edie Henner."

Edie wanted to drive a circuit of the park's closed lakes. She asked whether Ron cared to join her, since he was what she called a "camp type." He agreed to go. Waiting to meet with White and Moffett, he had little else to do.

"What did she want?" Jan's question had an edge.

"Wants me to drive around the park with her. See how camps on the other lakes compare with those on Menomini.

"Why?" she asked, frowning. "And why you?"

"Dunno why," he said. "Why me? I guess because of my interest in Camp Schoodic."

"Nothing else?"

Ron shook his head. He thought Edie might shed light on the strange doings at "his" camp but it seemed prudent not to say so.

***

The morning was bright but chilly when Edie and Ron began their tour. Ron's warmup jacket felt good. Mid-May is late spring in North Fork, but two growth zones earlier in the high country of Mill Run Park.

Ron had told Edie of his discovery in Schoodic's headquarters. Her muted reaction – "That's interesting," with no follow up – had puzzled him. Did she know about the activity in the camp? Or, as a park employee, did she prefer not to know? He had decided not to pursue the matter further.

By midday, they had visited two of the Park's smallest lakes. Edie had shown Ron reed-filled swimming areas and cabins in various stages of ruin. By each lake stood an imposing, hand-carved sign – "Algonquin," "Mandan" – whose varnish had long since shredded and whose bright pine had faded to dirty gray. Here and there, a stone recreation hall or a cabin upgraded in the 1970's or 80's looked promising for restoration, but no other camp had aged as gracefully as Schoodic, Herzl, and Schuetzen.

Edie stopped her four-by next to a sign at the entrance to Lake Abenaki's camp road. It advertised three camps. One was Luther, another Camp Sycamore, where she had camped and worked as a teen. Sycamore and the YMCA camp on the other side of the lake had still been occupied in 2008 when the lake was closed. "Want to go in?" she asked.

"Maybe later. I'd rather remember Camp Luther before…."

"Before the accident?" He nodded.

Pausing to look at a huge, circular patch of concrete at the head of Lake Abenaki, both Edie and Ron exclaimed, "The Pavvy!" The foundation, in almost perfect condition, was all that remained of a roller skating pavilion that both of them had enjoyed as teens. "It burned in 2005," Edie said. "Make a good helicopter pad, if there were anyone left on the lake to take out."

She drove on toward Lake Huron, but pulled over at a trail head half way between there and Abenaki. "A short walk in, there's a pretty little pond. You fancy lunch?"

"I didn't think to…"

71

"I did," she said, reaching behind the four-by's passenger seat and pulling out a knapsack.

Walking along the trail behind her, Ron added a few strokes to an emerging picture of Edie Henner. The Smokey Bear hat, big sun glasses, and loose, practical jeans made the tomboy impression that Jan had noticed. Today, a snug sweatshirt, lipstick, and a touch of mascara softened it. *How would her hair look*, he wondered, *if it escaped from the ranger hat.*

They had met several times, on the lake and in town, since their first encounter at the nature museum. Neither their conversations nor tidbits from Hoss at the barber shop had told Ron anything about Edie's personal life. At one point, he had noticed a pale spot on her sunburnt left hand where a ring might have been. He had asked, without thinking, "Married?"

Edie's terse reply – "Was, almost. Afghanistan." – answered his question without inviting a follow up. Ron inferred that the source of her ring was dead.

When they reached the little pond – Kettle Hole, she called it – Ron had an odd feeling that he had been there before, in a warmer season when the leaves were darker, but the view of the pond was unfamiliar. "Is there another trail to it?" he asked.

Edie paused from unpacking lunch and pointed to an open area on the far side of the pond. "Mine road. We used to hike it from Camp Sycamore. Older campers and staff came here to skinny dip."

Ron laughed. "Of course! We hiked here from Luther too. We called it 'Naked Lady Lake' because a bunch of our kids surprised some dippers there. Pity it's still too chilly for a swim!'" He regretted the quip at once when Edie frowned and blushed.

"I hope ham and cheese and a diet Coke work for you," she said. Sitting down beside him, she took off her hat, loosing a shimmer of long, wavy auburn hair that played well against her tanned face and olive green eyes. As the tomboy image vanished, Ron thought, *Maybe it's good that it's chilly!*

They had almost finished lunch and were enjoying the quiet beauty of the pond when Ron's cell phone yanked him back to reality. "I can't get used to it!" he exclaimed. "Nothing else works in the park, but there's still cell service!"

The message was a text: "Fire, southwest quadrant. Will advise."

"Dammit!" Ron exclaimed, pocketing the phone. "Most likely set by one of the firemen. Bastards!"

Edie, who had started to pack her knapsack, stopped. She jumped to her feet, put her hands on her hips, and glowered at him. "Bastards!" she exclaimed. "Most of those men had park jobs before the cutbacks!" Before Ron could react, she went on. "They get by as best they can. A few bucks for fighting a brush fire can mean a lot when you're trying to feed a bunch of kids on food stamps and road kill. You have no idea…."

Ron had started a fire himself. "Sorry! The barber told me…"

"Hoss should know better!" she snapped. "He's barely hung on since the lakes closed. Milltown's almost a ghost town, and it's not alone." She waved her arms north and south. "Purlin! Boxboro! Towns that just squeaked by with business from the park. Towns that are dying without it!"

"There's still the ski center," Ron said.

"Not enough!" she exclaimed. "Not half enough. Four months of pay to make up for eight without!"

Then, to Ron's surprise, she laughed. "The funny thing is that some of the guys who were laid off would have spent last year demolishing Schoodic and the other camps on Menomini, Abenaki, and the other small lakes."

Ron knew Menomini headed the state's hit list for demolition, but he hadn't thought of all the implications. "The ranger cabin?"

"You and Jan wouldn't be living there now!"

Edie tucked her hair in her hat, picked up her pack, and started down the trail to the car. Following her, Ron noticed something on one of her boots: A green smudge that was different – bluer – than the olive of her eyes. He had seen that color before, in Schoodic's nature building and on a paint can stored under its headquarters.

Turning to let Ron catch up, Edie noticed his startled expression. "Problem?" she asked.

"No. Just admiring your boots!"

For a moment, neither of them spoke. Then Edie grabbed Ron's arm and laughed. "Okay," she said, "there's someone you need to meet. Can you be at Camp Schuetzen tomorrow morning, say 10:30?"

Ron nodded. "I'll be there!"

14. Gus

"I have some business over at Camp Schuetzen," Ron told Jan at breakfast the next morning. "Don't wait lunch for me." He saw no reason to explain that his business involved Edie Henner.

Driving along the east side of Menomini, Ron had a feeling that the bag he had opened at lunch the day before contained more than one cat. He was about to meet another that might shed light on what was up at Camp Schoodic and why it seemed to involve him.

As he approached Camp Schuetzen, he saw two cars parked on its volleyball court. One was Edie's four-by, the other a white Mercedes sedan that dwarfed it. He parked, got out, and walked around the Mercedes. An S-class, it had enough scratches and dings to indicate hard use in what he took to be three or four years, but its Moroccan leather upholstery told him it had cost north of $100,000 new. A low number on its license plate and a parking sticker for the state capital implied that the owner was well connected as well as rich. Edie's lawyer father perhaps?

Ron walked past the camp's mess hall and down a path to the lake, drawn by voices at the dock. One voice was Edie's, the other masculine with a heavy German accent. The man was a head shorter than Edie, gray-haired, and heavy set. Ron guessed he was in his sixties or seventies. A red and black plaid shirt and patched jeans fit in the camp setting. A Tyrolean fedora with a chamois beard didn't, nor did a big green parrot that was perched on the man's shoulder.

"*Grüss Gott!*" the parrot squawked as Ron stepped onto the dock.

At the sound, the man turned and strode toward Ron, his eyes alight, his grin broadened by a droopy gray moustache. "Goot morning!" he boomed, pumping Ron's hand. "I am Schneider. You are Tyler, no? *Es freut mich sehr!*"

Ron nodded. Resisting a temptation to click his heels and bow, he settled for, "*Es freut mich auch!*"

"He speaks *Deutsch*!" Schneider exclaimed, beaming.

Edie laughed. "Anyone who gives German a try gets Grandpa Gus's vote!"

The tumblers clicked in Ron's mind. Schneider. Gus, short for August. Capital parking sticker. Of course! The stout, red-faced man who stood before him was the upstate senator who had raged against the park layoffs and lake closures.

A hero to students like Ron in 2008, he was better known to NoFo's professors for the 2004 Schneider Law, which had forced all state employees to unionize. Because neither he nor anyone else had thought to make an exception for professors, they had been swept, kicking and screaming, into a subdivision of the AFL-CIO. Many never forgave him.

Ron suppressed a grin as he recalled a cartoon in the campus newspaper. It showed a jackbooted soldier with a Kaiser moustache and spiked helmet carrying a squirming pig under one arm and a crumpled copy of the U.S. Constitution in the other hand. The pig referred to Schneider's other life as the state's wealthiest pig farmer.

"Let's get out of the wind," Edie said, turning her collar up. She led the men up the hill to the mess hall, whose lakeward side was open but sheltered by trees. On the way, she explained that Gus was one of the few Germans in New Westphal whose families had resisted pressure to anglicize their surnames. Some of his relatives, knowing that *Schneider* means tailor in English, had become Taylors. Müllers had morphed into Millers. Schneider bristled. "Cowards!" he exclaimed. "Like those silly Battenburgs who became Mountbattens!"

Gus had no doubt that his reputation as proudly German – "dumb Dutch," opponents said -- stood against him in the Senate, but he had rammed the Schneider Law through against opposition. He claimed it protected the university from the sort of penny-pinching that had squeezed the life out of Mill Run State Park. "I don't give up!" he exclaimed. "I am like Roy Roberts, that Irishman with the spider!"

Ron must have looked puzzled, for Edie laughed. "*Rob Roy*, Opa!" she said. "And he was Scottish!"

"Scottish, Irish. Whatever!" the old man growled.

The trio sat on benches in the mess hall for the next hour while Schneider reviewed the park's history and his efforts to reopen its lakes and revive its camps. Switching often between English and German, he painted a self-portrait that softened the demonic cartoon image but didn't quite erase it. Even after years of legislative defeats, he was hell bent to restore the park jobs, reopen the lakes, and save the camps.

Ron was sympathetic but skeptical. Edie saw his frown and bristled. "The conservative majority up in the capital wants to close the western half of the park for good," she said, "and the 'back to nature' lobby agrees with them." Her lip quivered. "Level the cabins! Fire what's left of the park staff! End it!"

It quickly became clear why Gus and Edie were passionate about Menomini's camps. Their family had spent ski weekends and summer vacations at Camp Schuetzen in the 1930's, before its leaders turned toward Hitler. Later, Edie's father, Paul Henner, and her uncle had attended and worked at Camp Schoodic. So had her older brother, Hannes. Although Edie camped and worked on Lake Abenaki, she had spent enough time on Menomini to get it into her blood. Since

77

Schoodic closed, Gus had watched over it and he, Edie, and Hannes had done things to spruce it up.

"Like the awful green paint?" Ron asked playfully, "And the new toilet paper holder?"

Edie blushed, then laughed. "You almost caught me that first night!"

"Were you trying to draw me in?" Ron asked.

Schneider guffawed. "Draw you in? *Keineswegs* – no way! She wanted to scare you off. She was afraid a city boy like you would report us for trespassing!"

"You were hard to discourage," Edie said. "It was just a game until…"

"Until?" Edie's hesitation and a glow on her cheeks told Ron she was trying to avoid defining a relationship that both of them were drawn to but feared.

Fortunately, Schneider broke the spell. "Until Editta – Edith – saw that you are one of us. You have the camps…" He struggled with English for a moment, then thumped his chest and concluded, "…*im Herz!* In the heart!"

Edie stood up. "It's past noon. Jan will wonder what became of you."

Schneider took Ron's hand again and looked at him intently. "*Danke*…thank you for coming! I hope we meet again."

"*Danke schön!*" the parrot squawked as they walked toward the cars.

"*Bitte schön!*" Ron replied, to Gus's delight.

78

***

Driving past the nature museum and the derelict Camp Lackawanna, Ron thought about Gus's words. He did indeed have camps *im Herz*, Luther as well as Schoodic. Luther was gone and its passing had scarred him.

By contrast, Camp Schoodic seemed to be just asleep. He had stood on the camp road below headquarters one day, closing his eyes, and imagining that its campers and counselors were out on day hikes. *They'll return at sundown*, he thought, *marching down the road and singing "We're happy when we're hiking...."* The thought had brought tears to his eyes.

Although he was already late for lunch, Ron pulled over at the Menomini overlook, got out and walked a few yards for a better view of the lake. To his left, he could see the ranger cabin and its garage. His mind turned to Jan. Already suspicious of his friendship with Edie Henner, she had become more so after the women met in the IGA. He had assured her that it was just friendship, but was it? He remembered Edie's gestures -- hugs, light touches on his arm, a playful peck on the cheek --- that had made him wonder if there was more to it on her side. Was there more on his?

He walked back to the car, started it, and backed onto CR-5. "She's just a friend!" he exclaimed. *For now* crossed his mind, but he banished it. "Forever!" he growled.

15. Mehring

In 2006, just before the recession made such ventures impossible, Milltown, Purlin, Boxboro and several smaller communities along Mill Run built the central school complex that stands at the south end of Milltown. The state picked up 90% of its cost and gave the new district generous terms for the rest.

As Jan had noted when she and Ron first visited Milltown, one building in the sprawling K-12 complex is a library. The Tylers were already well acquainted with it through Jan's volunteer work when Ron went there on the Saturday morning after his encounter with Gus Schneider. His mission was to pick up DVD's for the weekend while Jan shopped for a few things in the IGA.

Browsing through the library's extensive movie collection, Ron didn't notice a stooped, gray-bearded man who was perusing disks nearby, but the man noticed him. "You're pretty young to choose that one," he said. "Excuse me," he apologized, "but most people your age prefer Branagh's *Hamlet* to Olivier's."

Ron laughed. "Sir Ken has the edge for cinematography and Kate Winslet is a definite plus, but O had Jean Simmons!"

The man shifted several DVD's to his left hand and offered Ron his right. "Mehring," he said, "Bill Mehring. It was rude of me to intrude, but I'm so tired of my students pooh-poohing classic movies that it's a treat to meet a fan!"

"Ron Tyler. You teach?"

"Yep," Mehring said, "high school English. Been at it since the late Seventies. You?"

"I'm a grad student in English Literature at North Fork State, taking time out to finish a Master's thesis on an obscure colonial poet."

Mehring wrinkled his nose. "Prose man myself!"

"Me too," Ron said.

Mehring looked at Ron, his eyebrows raised. "Milltown seems like a strange place to work on a thesis."

"Blame the recession!" Ron exclaimed. "My wife and I lost our university jobs in January. We're living free – well almost – in a ranger cabin on Lake Menomini. I plan to start doctoral work in the fall."

"Ah! "You're the young man Edie Henner speaks of!"

"I hope she says good things," Ron said. He felt a flush rising in his cheeks and hoped it wasn't obvious. "Nice girl that."

"More than nice!" Mehring exclaimed. "She loves Mill Run Park like nobody else, Gus Schneider perhaps excepted. Says you're a fan too." The old man looked at his watch and frowned. "Nice meeting you, Ron, but Sally – my wife -- is waiting lunch for me. I hope we'll meet again."

"That's likely," Ron said. "Jan and I restock every week or so. The cabin's TV brings in mostly snow, but its disk player works just fine."

Ron shook Mehring's hand, walked to the librarian's desk, and put *Hamlet* and three other DVD's on it. "One week," the librarian reminded him as he fished out his library card, "but you know we're not too serious about fines!" As he turned to leave, she said, "I saw you talking to Bill Mehring."

"Nice fellow," Ron said. "Been teaching here almost forever!"

"He loves it!" she exclaimed. "You haven't met *Macbeth* till you've heard him read it! Did he tell you he's also Milltown's mayor? It's a tough job what with the layoffs and all."

"No, he didn't mention that."

***

Driving up 15A through Milltown, Ron had an odd feeling that his encounter with Mehring wasn't accidental. The old man probably knew who he was before he asked: No one has an ear to the ground like a small town mayor! And no one would be more interested in what Gus and Edie were up to in the park.

Jan was coming out of the IGA when Ron got there. He pulled into the parking lot, jumped out, and put two bags of groceries in the Honda's trunk.

"What did you get at the library?" Jan asked as they drove along CR-5 toward Lake Menomini.

"Olivier's *Hamlet* and some early episodes of *West Wing*. I also met Milltown's mayor."

"Bill Mehring?" Jan asked. "His wife is in the knitting group at church."

"Funny he didn't mention that. He said he had heard of me from Edie Henner."

Jan's frown told Ron that was more than she needed to know. They drove the rest of the way home in silence.

16. Jennifer's Birthday

After Harry Edwards's death, Jan and her brother took every opportunity to keep their mother from feeling abandoned. Jennifer's first Thanksgiving as a widow was strained because she insisted on trying to make it the all-flags-flying affair of the past. Christmas wasn't much different except for too much roast beef instead of too much turkey.

"Just don't bring it up," Ron told Jan on a late May morning as they passed the turnout for Purlin and continued down the freeway toward Blackwater and Jennifer's birthday party. "It" was politics, which could turn a family meal into World War III. Harry had been able to loosen his reins enough to swap biases with a liberal or moderate. Absent his gentling influence, Jennifer had lurched far to the right. She thought Newt Gingrich was a closet socialist and Sarah Palin deserved sainthood.

During four years at North Fork State, Jan and her brother had drifted to the left, though not as far as Ron had. After some dustups with Jennifer, all three learned to switch to admiring her watercolors whenever danger loomed.

"Stay off my pregnancy too," Jan said. By the end of May, her morning sickness had abated and other signs of her condition were not yet obvious, but Jennifer fretted about her being far from good medical help. She played that tune in more and more frequent phone calls, when she wasn't asking Jan when Ron would finish his schooling and "get a proper job."

"Dammit!" Ron growled. "Didn't you tell her that New Westphal has a new full service hospital, and it's less than an hour away? For emergencies, the Milltown Rescue Squad has a helicopter pad behind the high school."

"I did, but it didn't help. 'A bunch of pig farmers!' Mom said of New Westphal. She broke down at the idea of pregnant me in a helicopter."

Ron laughed. "Your mother thinks anything north of Blackwater is the jungle. Some of those pig farmers, Gus Schneider for one, are richer than many North Fork bankers! They paid off the new hospital with bonds and are building a new concert hall for the booming community college. A jungle indeed!"

"I think Mom is more worried about her own future than she is about mine."

Ron nodded. The sprawling Georgian mansion where the Edwardses had entertained dozens of Harry's colleagues and customers was now much too big for her. Two maids couldn't replace Harry, who had proudly fixed leaks, cracks, and sparking outlets. Nor could one young Mexican gardener maintain his putting green lawn and arboretum class shrubs and flower beds.

While Albert was preparing Jennifer's tax forms in 2009, he suggested that she downsize. She countered, "Why don't you and Marilyn just move in with me?" Albert warned Jan to add transplanting Mom to the list of landmines to be avoided.

By the time the Civic pulled into the winding, tree-lined drive that led to the Edwards mansion, Jan and Ron were ready to face dinner at Jennifer's huge, round, glass-topped mahogany dining table, which had seated twelve diners. The Tylers, Albert, and Albert's wife would have been more comfortable in the kitchen. ("We can always communicate with signal flags," Albert had whispered to Ron at Christmas.), but tradition demanded polished silver and pressed napkins. A gigantic ham (*One of Gus's?* Ron wondered.) would haunt Jennifer's freezer for months even after Marilyn and Jan took home huge CARE packages.

The birthday party was less tense than the Tylers feared. It helped that Marilyn announced over cocktails that she was pregnant too and would deliver shortly after Jan. A lively discussion of baby names carried the family through the soup course and well into the entrée. Then, just before dessert, Albert asked Jan, "Don't you guys have a lot of free time up there in the woods?"

"It's not that bad," Jan replied. "We have a TV. It brings in just three grainy channels on a good day, but it has a DVD slot." When Albert raised a brow, she added, "The school library has lots of DVD's."

Turning to Ron, Albert asked, "What do you do all day? Writing must be hard without a computer."

"Oh, I have a laptop and we get DSL through the phone line."

Albert's eyebrows rose again. "Who pays for the DSL? Isn't the lake closed?"

It was a reasonable question, but Ron fudged it. "I guess someone forgot to cancel phone service after the layoffs." He knew the right answer -- Gus Schneider – but wasn't inclined to mention the old Democrat for fear of setting off a Jennifer rant.

Albert shifted sail. Grinning, he asked, "What do you do for the park to earn the big bucks?"

"Oh, watch for fires and run off vandals."

"And he's adopted a camp," Jan said. As soon as the words left her mouth, she knew her toe was on a mine.

Jennifer's antennae went up. "He's done what?"

"Well, it's sort of the other way around," Ron explained. "The camp adopted me. I just do little things to tidy it up."

"I don't understand," Albert said. "Didn't the legislature condemn all the camps?"

"They voted for it. Haven't begun the job yet because of the layoffs."

Now Jennifer's wind was up. "Let me understand you, Ronald," she said coldly. "You're fooling around with a condemned camp instead of finishing your thesis?"

A hush fell over the big table. Ron winced, expecting a diatribe about irresponsible young husbands. Then Jan turned and pointed to a watercolor painting that hung over the mahogany sideboard. "Mom," she said, "I've always loved what you do with lilies!"

"Those are poppies!" Jennifer exclaimed. Then, softly, "Do you really like it?"

"I do! Paint one for us, please!"

Well played! Ron thought as a maid served coffee and the conversation returned to the safe ground of baby names.

17. The Verdict

On the morning after Jennifer's party, Ron went to the university to meet with his readers. "Very well done!" Sam White said, shaking Ron's hand. He was satisfied with Ron's final tweaks of the thesis, which included increasing type size and widening margins to create more pages and a thicker book. ("Everyone does that!" White had told him between drafts.)

When Ron expressed his fear that Professor Moffett would still insist that too little was known about Francois Luquer to justify an essay, much less a book, White erupted. "Nonsense, my boy! Think musically! A talented composer can take a few notes and build a great symphony. Who knew what Beethoven would make out of 'dit-dit-dit-dah?' "

Ron left White's office with two depressing thoughts. One was *I'm not Beethoven!* The other, which Moffett might have said, was *Beethoven knew the difference between a bit of gold that can be hammered thin to gild a cathedral and a chunk of lead that can't.*

White would sign off on the thesis in time to meet Harvard's deadline, just two weeks away. Now Ron had to face his second reader, whose office was at the other end of the sprawling humanities building. A secretary ushered him into Moffett's bookshelf-lined office and directed him to an arm chair in front of the professor's desk. An open copy of Ron's thesis lay atop a pile of papers on the desk.

"Professor Moffett will join you directly," the secretary said. "He's finishing a Ph.D. defense. Coffee or tea?"

"Neither, thanks." He was jittery enough to make a cup of hot liquid dangerous.

While he waited, Ron looked at the professor's bookshelves. Gaps in them marked tomes that had migrated to Moffett's desk or a groaning table by the window. He thought, *Will my office look like this twenty years from now?*

As Ron was pondering his future, the door opened and Moffett strode in. His tie was askew, his long salt and pepper hair rumpled. "Sorry to keep you," he said. "Miss Chiu passed her exam, but it was a near thing! Do you know her?"

Ron nodded. "I think we were in freshman English together."

Moffett sat down behind the pile of papers, pressed his fingers together, and stared at Ron from beneath heavy, gray eyebrows. Then he cleared his throat and asked, "Ronald – if I may be informal – how have you spent your time on Lake Menomini?" When it became obvious that Ron was too startled to answer the unexpected question, he restated it. "What do you do when you're not trying to write a story that isn't there?"

He's going to turn me down! Ron thought, his cheeks burning. *Goodbye, Harvard!* He started to stand up, but Moffett said, quietly, "I'm not finished." As Ron sat down again, he asked, "What inspires you, Francois Luquer?" Ron shook his head. "Library research?" *Where is this going?* Ron wondered, shaking his head again. "Teaching?" He nodded. "Writing?" Here, his nod was emphatic. "And…."

Still unsure why Moffett was grilling him, Ron was beginning to think, *What the hell!* He blurted, "Camping! The outdoors!"

Moffett leaned back in his chair, stared at Ron for an excruciating half minute, then chuckled. "Teaching. Writing. The outdoors." He leaned forward. His brow was furrowed, but his eyes gleamed. "Why would someone with your interests and talents want to go to Harvard? To learn how to be another Sam White?" He sat back, pressed his fingers together again, and said, "Our students tell me you're a gifted teacher. Your thesis is pathetic – much ado about not much – but it is very well written. Indeed, every page cries 'Writer!'"

Thoroughly confused, Ron clenched his fists, waiting for the verdict. What came after another agonizing silence startled him. "I'll sign off on your thesis before Harvard's deadline," Moffett said, "but on one condition. You must agree to spend the next two weeks asking yourself whether Harvard and academia are really where you belong."

It took Ron a moment to absorb what Moffett had proposed. Then he mumbled, "Thank you, sir. I accept the condition."

"Grand!" Moffett exclaimed. "Let me know what you decide." He stood up, shook Ron's trembling hand, and gestured toward the door, signaling that the audience was over.

"Thank you again," Ron said and left the office. As he walked to the humanities parking lot, he mopped his forehead and loosened his drenched shirt collar. Had he won or lost? On one hand, he was relieved: Both readers would approve his thesis, stamp him "M.A." and send him off to Harvard. On the other, Moffett had raised troubling questions that Sam White should have asked two years earlier: "Who are you? Who do you want to be?"

Ron's nemesis had become his mentor.

***

Driving north on Route 15 the next morning, Jan was chatty. "The party wasn't so bad, was it? Isn't it neat that Marilyn is pregnant too? Our baby will have a cousin!"

Ron was subdued. He had told Jan about Moffett's decision to sign off on his study of Luquer. He hadn't shared the professor's command to think carefully before he accepted Harvard's offer.

Listening to Jan's upbeat chatter, Ron realized they were no longer flying wing tip to wing tip. Going to Harvard in the fall – their wide, straight road – would please her and Jennifer, but at what cost? He had less than two weeks to answer that question and make his – their -- decision. And he needed to tell Jan what his involvement with Edie, Gus, and Camp Schoodic was and wasn't.

It would be a tense time in the ranger cabin on Lake Menomini.

18. Decision

On a rainy Monday a week before Harvard's deadline, Ron washed the breakfast dishes, turned off the grainy CBS news that began every morning in the ranger cabin, and sat down across the kitchen table from Jan. "We need to talk," he said.

Pretending to be shocked, Jan wailed, "You're leaving me!"

Ron laughed, more from surprise than amusement. "No, not ever, but I've made a decision that will affect all three of us."

"Harvard?" Jan knew its deadline was just days away. She also knew Ron had struggled for months with a feeling that his Master's thesis was a waste of time.

"That's part of it," he said. "There was more to my sit down with Professor Moffett than I've shared with you. I made a promise in return for his signature on my thesis."

"A promise?"

"He urged me, before I accept Harvard's offer, to ask myself whether I'm really cut out for an academic career."

"And?" Jan fidgeted with a teaspoon .

"I'm not, at least not now. I like teaching and writing but I really hated those long days in musty libraries. And I love – need – camping, hiking, the outdoors."

Jan was quiet for a moment, still fingering the spoon. Then she asked, "Did the camp have anything to do with your decision? And the ranger lady?"

"Schoodic yes, Edie no. The camp played on old memories, some bad but mostly good."

Jan laughed. "Tell me about the bad ones! My shins are bruised from when you act out your nightmares!" Then she frowned. "But what about Edie?"

Ron pushed away from the table and shook his head. "Edie and her grandfather passed on their passion for the lakes and camps. They showed me how much damage was done when they were closed."

"And...?" Jan's half closed eyes and downturned lips told Ron she was afraid Edie's passion, and his, went beyond Camp Schoodic. It didn't help that he answered her slowly, choosing his words carefully.

"Edie and I are friends," he said, "the best kind, with no agenda beyond the interests that brought us together." Seeing that Jan's eyes were moist, he stood up, walked around the table, and gripped her shoulders. "Not Edie Henner, nor anyone else, can separate you and me! Wherever we go, whatever we do, it will be together!"

Jan was still for a moment. Then she reached up and squeezed his hands. "Okay, Ronnie, what's next?"

"I'll send Harvard a 'Thank you, but...'" letter, e-mail Professor Moffett, and phone Sam White to tell him about my decision." He paused for a moment to wipe his own moist eyes. "That will be a painful call!"

"Then?"

"I'll start looking for a teaching job. Maybe Bill Mehring can give me some leads."

"And Schoodic?" Jan asked.

"We have this cabin till year's end. I'll keep my ranger job and do some more handyman stuff at the camp."

"With Edie?" Jan asked. Her lingering cobwebs of doubt were obvious. Ron shrugged. He had said all he could say. Only time could brush those cobwebs away.

19. Spinnaker

A few mornings after Ron's conversation with Jan, he and Edie were standing outside Camp Schoodic's headquarters. "You'll have to break it," Edie said. "It" was a padlock on the building's front door.

"I'm uneasy about this," Ron said. "It's one thing to nail a few boards on tent platforms and fix sinks in a washhouse. It's another to break into a building."

Edie laughed. "*Whose* building? The church group that ran Schoodic gave up the ghost soon after it closed!"

"Still...."

"If someone asks me about the door, I'll tell 'em kids did it." Laughing again, Edie added, "Maybe say they tied up the lake foreman!"

Ron took a pry bar that he'd found under the building and went to work on the lock. The hasp pulled away from the weathered door post easily. "See?" Edie said. "Didn't even need nitro!"

The building's heart was a massive stone fireplace. On its mantel stood a photograph of the long dead Lutheran bishop who had founded Camp Schoodic in the 1930's, a cavalry bugle, and a carved, rainbow-colored peace pipe. Like the graces in the mess hall, these abandoned artifacts testified to a quick departure. Why had no one thought to take them?

Edie ignored the fireplace and headed straight to a three drawer file cabinet in the corner of the office. She pulled out a drawer labeled "Campers," withdrew a stack of manila folders, and put them on a table next to the file cabinet. "Pull up a chair," she said. "Look at the camper lists, working backward from 2000. See if any names ring bells."

"Bells?"

"Anyone who's prominent now, in Milltown or North Fork." She pulled out the cabinet's second drawer, labeled "Schoodic Herald." "I'll look through old camp newspapers."

It seemed like a dreary way to spend a nice summer morning, but Ron went along. Edie sat on a stool nearby. When Ron recognized a name, he told her. When one was familiar to her, she told him. Their consultations for the 1990's and 80's were few. "Eric Henner, 1976 camper list!" Ron sang out.

"My father's brother," Edie replied, but in a way that indicated disinterest. Ron found no one else of note in the '70's files.

"Just what are we looking for?" he asked as he returned one stack of folders to the cabinet and pulled out another.

"Someone who might be able to help us save the camps. Here's a prospect," she said, passing a faded copy of Schoodic's newspaper to him. "Look at the byline."

"Bill Mehring! He edited the camp paper in 1966!"

"Right!" Edie said. "Bill's on our side and he has pull, but I'm afraid a schoolteacher couldn't give us much financial help. Look back a few more years."

Ron glanced at his watch. He was about to tell Edie he had to leave for lunch when a name near the bottom of the 1957 camper list caught his eye: "Spinnaker, Eustace." He recalled seeing part of that surname – SP...N...KER – on the weathered side of an abandoned mill building south of town. "Spinnaker!" he exclaimed.

"Bingo!" Edie slammed her file drawer shut. "The Spinnakers owned the biggest textile mill in Milltown, maybe the whole state.

They squirreled away enough money during the boom years to keep their estate after the industry crashed."

"A prospect?" Ron asked.

"Maybe, but old Eustace has been a recluse since his wife died a decade ago. Has food delivered from the IGA. Never shows up for town meetings."

Ron replaced his folders, closed the "Campers" drawer, and turned to leave. "See you tomorrow," Edie said, adding with a wry smile, "if Jan can spare you."

Ron shook his head. "Can't do. Maybe the day after."

***

Spinnaker haunted Ron overnight and through a morning of cleaning up in and around the ranger cabin. Because the wood pile was almost flat and nights were still chilly, he spent the day hauling, cutting, and splitting deadfall. It was late afternoon when he got back to the cabin.

Might Bill Mehring be able to tell him more about Eustace Spinnaker? Ron reckoned the teacher would be home from school by 4:30 and called him then. He got his voicemail, having forgotten that Tuesday was the teacher's afternoon with the Shakespeare Club.

Mehring returned Ron's call after supper. "Sure I know Eustace. Once on a time we were on the town board together."

"Do you think he'd talk to me if he knew I'm interested in his old camp?"

"I'll ask him," Mehring said, "but he has seen no one but delivery boys for the last few years."

***

Mehring arranged a meeting with Spinnaker on Friday morning, June 25th. In preparation for it, Ron spent Thursday browsing through town documents in the library. The most interesting was a large aerial photo of Milltown and the broad valley in which it lies. It and old newspapers filled in some blanks in Will Orville's history.

Like Menomini's valley but wider and deeper, that of Mill Run was cut by a vigorous stream, then sculpted by a moving glacier during the Ice Age. When the glacier melted some 10,000 years ago, it left the creek with a steep gradient and waterfalls that made it ideal for mills.

The aerial photo contains clues to Milltown's commercial ups and downs. A beehive during the iron years, the town sagged in the 1880's, then rose to become a textile center in the 1890's and the early 1900's. It declined again in the 1930's when cheaper labor drew most of the textile companies to the Carolinas and Georgia.

The photo shows the remains of three mills south of town, the largest Spinnaker's. East of Mill Run and the Route 15 freeway stands a double row of almost identical company houses. Examining the mill grounds in the photo with a magnifying glass, Ron made out raised roadbed and other evidence of tracks that once connected the mills to the main rail line to North Fork. He also identified the abutments of a long gone bridge across Mill Run, relics of the narrow gauge railroad that had carried loads of pig iron from mountain furnaces like the one south of Lake Menomini.

Mehring had told Ron that Milltown and other communities up and down the valley were already failing when, in 2006, the state moved Route 15 across the river and widened it to four lanes. Main Street and other main streets were left to wither.

Because Spinnaker's estate lies west of town, Ron trained his magnifying glass on that part of the photograph. The pattern of north-south ridges and valleys that underlies the western half of Mill Run State Park reappears there. Most of the upland is wooded, but Ron noticed a half dozen cleared areas, some of them tens of acres across. Each area is an estate with an imposing mansion. Some of the estates include barns and other outbuildings. One has a race track.

The ridge top estates testify to the enormous wealth that mine and mill owners accumulated during Milltown's glory days. Ron now understood why a battered sign on a derelict building two blocks west of Main Street boasts, "Opera House."

Shot in the 1980's, the aerial photo exaggerates Milltown's wealth in 2010. "Most of the mansions are shuttered now," Mehring had told Ron, "their aging owners living more modestly in Florida or the Carolinas. Some have just been abandoned to raccoons and dry rot."

"But Spinnaker's estate survived?"

"Yes," Mehring replied. "Spin Drift made it through the Depression because Eustace's Scots grandfather, Elbert, moved his fortune to Campbell soup and cash after an industry-wide textile strike in 1928. If he had acted a year or two later, his mansion would be abandoned too."

***

Ron had the aerial photo and Milltown's history in mind on Friday morning as he drove south on Main Street, then turned right on the aptly named Ridge Road. "Spin Drift is at the end," Mehring had told him, adding, "Don't tire Eustace. He's pushing 70 and a bit fragile."

As Ron drove up the narrow, serpentine road through stands of pine, oak, and hemlock, he passed several potholed and weedy side roads that led to abandoned estates. The rusty sign by one -- "Bassett"-- recalled a family that prospered in wool after its iron mines played out but went under after the 1928 strike. Ron fancied that the bullet holes in the sign were, as old man Bassett claimed at the time, "communist inspired."

A long, avenue of overgrown pines atop the first ridge west of town led to a turnaround and, beyond that, a looming, mass of granite capped by turrets and a slate roof. Ivy scrambled up Spin Drift's walls, outrunning huge rhododendrons and Andromeda that obscured the mansion's first floor windows and threatened the second as well. Ragged columns of holly bracketed the steps to the mansion's front door, making it almost invisible. The rampant greenery put Ron in mind of the briar rose hedge in "Sleeping Beauty."

As he got out of the Civic, he noticed a vista of Mill Run's valley and the state park beyond it that must have been stunning before overgrown oaks and poplars curtained it off. While he was trying to get a glimpse the town through the trees, dark thoughts crossed his mind. *Why am I here? What do I -- well what does Edie -- want from an old man who obviously prefers to be left alone? Just talk about camp*, he thought as he climbed the mansion's stone steps.

Unable to find a doorbell amid the tangle of holly, he slammed a gargoyle-faced knocker that glared at him. After what seemed like five minutes, a lock turned and the massive oak door creaked open. Expecting a liveried butler, Ron was startled to face a stooped, white-haired man in a plaid shirt, dirty overalls, and yellow garden boots. He was months overdue for a haircut and his white mustache drooped at one end. Fresh mud on his wellies told Ron that he had been working outside. The gardener, Ron assumed.

"Good morning, sir," he said. "I'm Ronald Tyler. Mr. Mehring suggested that I visit Mr. Spinnaker to talk about Camp Schoodic."

The old man nodded slightly, stood back, and pointed a trembling index finger down the mansion's center hall. "Library, second door on the right," he whispered. "Mr. Spinnaker will join you shortly."

Ron followed the old man's instructions and found himself in a huge room, surrounded by crowded book shelves that almost reached its ten foot ceiling. In one corner stood a movable ladder and a long-poled grabber like the one the IGA's clerks use to fetch cans from high shelves. A grand piano stood at one end of the library, a long table with eight chairs at the other. All of the furniture but the piano was covered by sheets.

In the middle of the room, on a deep-piled oriental rug, stood a small, round card table surrounded by four burgundy leather arm chairs. Two of the chairs were covered with sheets. The others, on opposite sides of the table, were bare and dust-free, suggesting they had just been uncovered. A decanter of wine and two glasses stood on the table.

While Ron waited for Spinnaker, he walked to the piano and opened it, resisting an urge to strike a key or two to see if it was in tune. The piano seemed to be of the present. The rest of the room's furnishings, like the overgrown shrubs and trees outside, spoke of things once loved but long neglected.

Three ornately framed photographs stood on the piano. One, on the left, showed a pretty, middle-aged woman kneeling next to a bed of blooming iris. Another, in the middle, showed a man in his late twenties dressed in the blue uniform of an Air Force captain.

Ron was glancing at a little boy in the third picture when a rustle behind him told him he wasn't alone. He turned and was startled to face the old man who had greeted him at the front door, but in jeans instead of overalls and sandals rather than boots. The man walked toward him unsteadily, his trembling hand extended. "You're Tyler," he said. "I'm Spinnaker. Didn't expect you so soon. Got lost in Ellen's garden!"

For a moment, Spinnaker squinted at Ron through cataract-dimmed blue eyes. "Have we met before?"

"I don't think so," Ron replied, though his host also looked familiar.

"Oh well, sit down," Spinnaker said, settling into one of the easy chairs. As Ron sat in the other, he pushed the decanter toward him. "Is it too early in the day for a nip of sherry?"

More at ease, Ron grinned. "It's only eleven, but past noon somewhere!"

"You pour," the old man said. "Damned Parkinson's makes me get more outside a glass than in it!"

Spinnaker leaned back in his chair, looked at Ron sharply, and asked, "What's a young fellow like you doing on a dead lake?" He quizzed Ron for the next half hour, during which his hard-headed business side became obvious. When Ron told him how Jan had resisted his evidence that someone was taking care of Camp Schoodic, he nodded and said, "I'd have voted with her!" When Ron said he admired Gus Schneider's dogged campaign to restore the lakes and camps, he laughed. "Old fool! It was high hopes like his that cost my grandfather's friends their mills in 1929!"

Ron's cheeks burned. There was no way this nasty old man would help them on a mission that he saw as absurd!

Then Spinnaker leaned forward. "Sentimental old Schneider wants to bring back the glory days of camping," he said. "His hippie granddaughter bleeds for unemployed park workers." He stared at Ron. "But what's in their crusade for you? Did you go to Camp Schoodic?" Before Ron could reply, he answered his own question. "Of course not! You were probably too young when it closed. Like my grandson."

"No," Ron said. "I went to Camp Luther, over on Lake Abenaki." At this, Spinnaker stiffened, glared at him for a moment, and struggled to pull himself out of his chair. "I thought I recognized you!" he exclaimed. "You were at the inquest!" Suddenly, Ron remembered the withered old man who had sat in the back row of the gallery, sobbing as the coroner announced his verdict.

"Come with me!" Spinnaker commanded. Ron fought back tears as the old man led him to the piano. "The young man in the middle picture is – was – my son, Edward. Killed in Afghanistan, plane crash, just after Ellen…died." His voice trailed off in a long sigh as he stared at the woman's picture.

Ron didn't need to be told who the boy in the third picture was. Seeing it up close, he recognized one of the faces that had haunted his dreams for six years. He could hold his tears back no longer. "I'm so sorry," he sobbed. "Forgive me!"

Spinnaker turned to face him. "Forgive *you!*" he exclaimed, shaking a finger at him. "Forgive you for what? For an accident?" He shook his head angrily as tears poured down his cheeks.

"I meant…." Ron said.

The old man wasn't listening. "I'm the one who needs forgiveness!" he exclaimed. "I loved Camp Schoodic as a boy, always hoped my son would love it too. I was heartbroken when Eddie went to basketball camp instead." He pulled a handkerchief from his jeans

102

and dabbed at his eyes. "To be sure my grandson would go to Schoodic, I filled his head with camp stories: hiking, swimming, fishing, and pranks."

Spinnaker paused to blow his nose. "Where was I?" he asked, briefly disoriented. Then he resumed his story. "Eddie Jr. loved to hear how another boy and I liked to hide under the dock during buddy checks to scare the lifeguards. Schoodic was gone by the time he was old enough for camp, so I sent him to Camp Luther"

The old man's tears began to flow again as he took the boy's picture and clutched it to his chest. "I *told* him about that prank over and over!" he sobbed. "*I told him!*"

Crying too, Ron gently took the boy's picture and returned it to the piano. He put an arm around Spinnaker's shoulder, led him back to the round table, and poured some more sherry. When they were both more composed, the old man reached across the table and took Ron's hand. "Thank you for coming," he said. "I needed to tell that story to someone."

Ron squeezed his hand. "I needed to hear it."

***

"So you met Spinnaker?" Edie asked the next day as she and Ron were replacing floor boards on a tent platform.

"Yes."

"And?"

"You set me up!" Ron exclaimed. "It would have been helpful to know about his grandson."

"Would you have gone to Spin Drift if you knew?

103

"Probably not."

Edie moved a piece of flooring into position and held it while Ron drove in four nails. "Do you think he'll help us?" she asked.

"Hard to say." Ron laughed. "Eustace called Gus a sentimental old fool and you a hippie bleeding heart." He savored her scowl for a moment, then added, "But that was before we recognized each other."

Edie tapped her foot impatiently. "So will he help or won't he?"

"We'll invite him when we meet to plan strategy. Then we'll find out whether he still has the Schoodic virus."

20. "A Matter of Some Urgency"

"Phone for you," Jan called out the kitchen window one morning in late June. Ron put down the hedge shears he had been using to tidy up shrubs and went inside. "McManus," Jan whispered and handed the phone to him.

It took Ron a moment to make the connection between the caller and the Park Commission, for he hadn't spoken with Jack McManus since the Tylers first visited the lake. He sounded agitated, and background noise told Ron he was outdoors, on a pay or cell phone. Were he and Jan about to be evicted?

"Mr. Tyler," McManus said, barely audible over the background, "you're involved in a move to reverse the state's decision to close the small lakes in Northfield Park and raze the camps."

"I'm not!" Ron protested. Edie had warned him to keep quiet around state officials, for the sake of his job and hers.

"You are!" McManus's said angrily. "Never mind how I know! The important thing is something is up that you and your friends need to know about."

"What's that?"

"Because of the economic upturn this spring, the state has decided to rehire two dozen of the laid off park workers."

"That's great news!" Ron exclaimed.

"No, it's not!" McManus said. "Their jobs will be temporary and…"

"Better than nothing!" Ron interrupted..

"Let me finish!" McManus cried. "The men's job -- their only job -- will be to level all the camp buildings, to finish returning the western half of the park to wilderness!"

Ron was too stunned to respond. *Once the buildings are gone....*

"Are you still there?" McManus asked.

"Yes."

"Now, forget that you heard this from me. Oh, and good luck to you and your friends!"

***

"Pick up! Pick up!" Ron fumed. Usually Edie was easy to reach on her cell phone. This morning, even her voice mail was turned off. Then he remembered that she had gone to the capital for a weekend with her family. He called 411, got a number for her parents' home in Blackwater, and had the operator dial it.

"Henner here." The lawyer's deep baritone sounded professional: pleasant but firm.

"Mr. Henner, I'm Ronald Tyler, a friend of Edie's. I need to reach her as quickly as possible."

"Ah yes, Ron, she speaks of you often. May I tell her what this is about?"

Ron squirmed. Should he tell the lawyer what McManus had told him in confidence? He decided to put one toe in the water. "It's about Camp Schoodic, a matter of some urgency."

"Edie's shopping in the city with her mother," Henner said." I'll have her call you when they get back."

106

Ron thanked him. He was about to hang up when the lawyer added, "By the way, what you, Edie, and my father-in-law want to do will take guts. Let me know if I can help!"

Obviously, Henner was already in the picture! Ron told him about McManus's tip and the threat that there would soon be no camps left to fight for. "We'll need a lawyer," he said.

"You have one!" Henner exclaimed. "*Pro bono*, of course," he added to Ron's relief. "Step one is to verify McManus's story, step two to get a stay to prevent the demolition from going forward. I'll get to work on those things."

"What's next," Ron asked, "and how can I help?".

"Someone in the valley towns should call a meeting of those who were hurt by the layoffs and lake closures – the stakeholders."

"Edie would be my first choice for that," Ron said, "but she and I are park employees, like McManus. We need someone from outside, someone with political clout."

"How about Milltown's mayor? Moore, isn't it, or Mairs?"

"Bill Mehring, I'll ask him to call a meeting and invite the mayors of Purlin and Boxboro to attend. Their towns have been hurt as much as Milltown."

"Great!" Henner was warming to the task. "And the media! And, of course, Milltown's assemblyman and senator!"

After Ron hung up, he realized that he hadn't suggested inviting Eustace Spinnaker to the meeting, perhaps because it wasn't clear where the frail old man would fit in their scheme, if he fit at all.

***

Mehring grabbed the ball and ran with it as Ron had hoped he would. "We'll meet in Milltown's traffic court," he said when they spoke the next day. "Let's say 7 p.m. next Thursday. That work for you?"

Ron laughed. "I'll check my busy schedule!"

"Our first gathering should be small," Mehring said. "You and I, Gus Schneider, Edie, Paul Henner, and the mayors of Purlin and Boxboro." He thought for a moment. "And Eustace. He usually avoids town events, but I'll invite him anyway."

"The press?" Ron asked. "And legislators?"

"Henner has thought better about that. He thinks we should run silent until we know just what we're doing."

"What do you need from me?" Ron asked.

"Between now and next week, think of arguments for and against rehiring staff, re-opening the lakes, and saving the camps. Write up talking points, pro and con. You and I can meet next Tuesday morning to create an agenda for the meeting."

No sooner had Ron put down the phone when it rang again. "I've verified McManus's report," Henner said. "Justice Brant of the Fifth Circuit is willing to consider staying demolition of the camps, but he'll need a brief from us. I can work on that after we meet with the mayors."

"Good news?" Jan asked Ron after he hung up. His eyes were brighter, his smile wider than she had seen since they left North Fork.

"Very good news!" he exclaimed. He hugged her, but gently in deference to the baby. "I have a *writing* job!"

"Unpaid, of course!" she said with a wry smile.

"Of course," he replied. "*Pro bono!*"

21. A Tennis Match

Four days before his Tuesday meeting with Mehring, Ron was hunched over his laptop at the kitchen table. He pecked away furiously for a few minutes, then took a swig of coffee, squeezed his temples, and resumed his assault on the keyboard.

Jan, who was knitting a baby sweater by the fireplace, had seen Ron's performance many times, when he was wrestling with his thesis and the decision to pass up Harvard. "Have you figured out where you fit in all this?" she asked when he got up for a bathroom break.

"Not quite," he replied. "Right now, I'm playing legal tennis."

"Tennis? With whom?"

Ron laughed. "With myself! I have to build two cases: one for reopening the lakes and another for closing them once and for all."

Jan laughed. "Sounds schizo!"

"It is, and I have to get it done by Tuesday morning for a meeting of the mayors on Thursday night."

Ron had mined the *North Fork Herald's* on-line archives for reports on the legislature's decision to close the lakes. He had learned that although Gus Schneider was the loudest defender of the small lakes and the park workers, he wasn't alone. Bert Synstrom, who represented Milltown and the other valley communities in the Senate, had spoken up for the workers. Other upstate legislators had echoed him in the Assembly.

Most of the pressure to close the lakes had come from downstate. Jake Foster, who had represented the wealthy North Fork suburbs for forty years and now presided over the Senate, had written the bill to lay off staff. He had described it as "a small step forward in very hard times." Rejecting Synstrom's humane appeal, he had shaken his white mane, raised his fist, and roared, "The state's fiscal health has to take precedence over the inconvenience of a few workers!"

Ron's cheeks burned. *"Inconvenience!"* he growled. "So what if Milltown and Purlin wither as long as North Fork's bankers prosper!" He pushed away from the table, walked to the stove, and poured a fresh cup of coffee. *Hold the anger*, he thought. *Stick to facts.* An important one was that the dollars saved by dismissing 75 park workers were probably few and more than offset by increased welfare payments and the failure of businesses in the valley communities. *Is that true?* Ron wondered. *Proof needed! Numbers!*

Foster had many allies in the legislature and the state's business community, but Schneider, Synstrom and their colleagues had strong support from upstate mayors and the civil service employees union. That coalition might have blocked the layoffs if support for them hadn't come from environmentalists. Green-4-Ever, an organization with thousands of online members, had circulated a petition "to make Mill Run State Park's western lakes forever wild." Playing on popular concern for endangered species, the petition promised them "a safe haven within our state."

Drilling down on Green-4-Ever's website and Facebook page, Ron learned that both the petition and a passionate statement that was read to the legislature had been written by Green-4's zealous president, M. Armin Baum.

In a Senate hearing on the layoffs, Gus Schneider had called Baum and his Green-4 followers *"verdammte* tree huggers." The slur, widely quoted in print and on TV news, had hurt Gus's case more than Baum's. It also made Ron wince. Passionate about conservation since his camping days, he shared Green-4's commitment to protecting the shrinking wilderness. He had been delighted when the organization won a suit to prevent clear-cutting on state land.

111

Ron squeezed his forehead again and chuckled. "Something funny?" Jan asked.

"Yeah. Here I am, a card-carrying greenie, arguing against restoring a patch of wilderness!"

It was Jan's turn to laugh. "Playing both sides of the net!"

Ron settled back at his laptop and typed, "The small lakes and their group camps give children first-hand experience of nature as no museum or zoo can. Those kids (*Kids like me!* he thought) will, when grown, vote to preserve it." He printed out what he had written and showed it to Jan. "It's a hook!" he exclaimed. "In lobbying to close the lakes and raze the camps, Green-4-Ever voted against its own future!"

It took Ron only a moment to see that the hook was barbless. All but a handful of the park's group camps had failed years or decades ago. Did Camp Schoodic's sponsors still exist? Or Herzl's? "If the camps were spared, would they be used?" he whispered. "How many could re-open without major repairs? Who would pay for those repairs?"

Jan put her knitting down, got up, and stood behind Ron. "You're squeezing your forehead again and talking to yourself."

He looked up from his laptop and laughed. "It's one tough match. For every good argument, there's a good counter-argument!"

Would the camps be used? Interest in the environment had surged in recent years, driven by worry about climate change. There would still be kids like Ed Spinnaker who preferred a basketball or computer camp, but Ron thought -- well, hoped -- more boys and girls would be like Eustace's camp-hungry grandson.

"Hoped? Hoped?" Ron blurted, imagining craggy old Jake Foster, glowering and shaking his mane at the wishy-washy answer.

"Playing both sides of the net is exhausting!" he muttered. He paused for a sip of coffee, but it had gone cold. "Oh, for a microwave!" he growled.

"I'll brew more," Jan said. She put her knitting down again, filled the percolator and put it on the stove. Looking out the kitchen window, she asked, "Have you noticed that the marigolds are in bloom and the lilies are budding?"

Ron stood up, stretched, and joined her at the window. "I hope the deer leave your garden alone," he said. He walked back to the table, picked up his cell phone, and dialed it.

"Who are you calling?"

"Mehring"

"Bill," he said when the mayor picked up, "I think we'll be on firm ground Thursday if we focus on economic arguments for rehiring the park employees. We need hard data on how many people and businesses were affected by the layoffs in Milltown, Purlin, and Boxboro."

"People will be easy," Mehring said. "There are records of the number on public assistance before and after the firings." He thought for a moment, then said, "It's harder to estimate business losses. Might have to count 'for lease' signs."

"How about sales tax records?"

"Right!" Mehring exclaimed. "I'll get my secretary going on that and urge the other mayors to do the same."

"Bill," Ron said, "I'm a lot less confident about our case for saving the camps. If Wild-4-Ever weighs in again, we may be in trouble."

Mehring thought for a moment then said, "Other environmental groups might be more sympathetic to the camps. I'll nose around, but I'm not optimistic: Such outfits tend to support each other." He chuckled.

"What?"

"It would be bad news if we got Friends of Forests interested and they voted with Wild-4-Ever!"

"Right," Ron said. "I'll just make the best case I can. See you Tuesday." He put the phone in his pocket and closed his laptop.

"Tennis game finished?" Jan asked.

"Not quite, but I think I am – we are -- winning."

22. Déjà vu

When Ron walked into Milltown's police court at 6:30 on Thursday night, his eyes widened and his hands shook. He recognized the room: the judge's raised dais, the tables below it where defendants and their lawyers would sit, the witness stand and the tiered rows of seats in the spectators' gallery. The tables had been pushed together, but the scene was otherwise as Ron remembered it from the coroner's inquest. He glanced at the gallery expecting to see Eustace Spinnaker, but the old man wasn't there.

Bill Mehring was already seated at one end of the long table, shuffling papers that included the agenda that he and Ron had put together on Tuesday. Mehring had changed almost none of Ron's talking points. "You should think about getting a law degree!" he said. Then, more soberly, "Why not take notes tonight, in anticipation of writing a report?"

"Way ahead of you!" Ron replied, pulling out a tiny recorder that he had used during his research on Francois Luquer.

The agenda was short and simple. Paul Henner would summarize his findings. Then Mehring would ask the other mayors about their towns' experience since the layoffs. When the three mayors were firmly committed to trying to reverse the layoffs and reopen the lakes, the group would go through Ron's talking points.

Henner walked in a few minutes before seven, accompanied by his father- in- law and Edie. "*Guten Abend!*" Gus Schneider boomed.

"*Grüss Gott!*" Ron replied, relieved to see that Gus had left his chatty parrot at home. Edie gave Ron a sisterly peck on the cheek then took a seat in the front row of the gallery.

"Why not join us?" Mehring asked her.

She shook her head. "I'm a park employee, officially not here. I'm also deaf and dumb, so your secrets are safe."

At seven, two more people arrived. "Hello, Jim!" Mehring exclaimed. "Hi, Mary!"

"Evening, Bill!" James Wetherly, a middle-aged insurance agent with full, rosy cheeks, a broad smile, and a broader frame, had been Purlin's mayor for two terms, elected during the futile struggle against the relocation of Route 15. A moderate Republican, he was a fiscal conservative whose gay son had pulled him leftward on social issues.

Mary Strathmore, a high school biology teacher, was the new mayor of Boxboro, a village twelve miles up the valley from Milltown. In her early thirties and petite, she had bright blue eyes, long blond hair, and dimpled cheeks that made her look younger. (Ron imagined the 15-year-old boys in her class struggling to stay focused on their microscopes!) A Democrat, Mary was as far to the left of center on economic issues as Jim Wetherly was to the right.

Because Mehring had told the other mayors what Paul Henner had accomplished, the lawyer's summary was brief. The only question, from Wetherly, was "How sure are you that the temporary demolition jobs won't lead to permanent work?"

"As sure as anything can be in the capital!" Henner replied. "Once the five lakes are closed for good, the men won't be needed." Because that answer seemed to satisfy Wetherly, the meeting moved on to how the layoffs had affected the valley communities.

"It's hard to separate the effects of the layoffs from those caused by moving Route 15," Mehring said. The other mayors nodded. "However, we know that forty Milltown men and women lost their jobs when the state closed the lakes. After their unemployment insurance ran out, all but three went on public assistance."

"What became of the others?" Mary Strathmore asked.

"They moved away. Counting dependents, the layoffs affected about 125 people." Mehring noticed the other mayors exchanging frowns. "Right," he said. "that's not many, only about 5% of our 2500 citizens. But that's not the whole story. A comparison of sales tax receipts before and a year after the layoffs shows a 15% drop. Our IGA lost a bit more than 20% in income."

Mehring paused to let the statistics sink in, then turned to Wetherly, whose town lies fifteen miles south of Milltown. "Jim, how do Purlin's numbers square with ours?"

"We're a bit bigger than Milltown, about 3200 people, with only 25 layoffs. Between 75 and 100 people were affected directly."

He shuffled some papers in front of him. "Bill, the Route 15 move hit us hard," he said, "so we were already in trouble. I'd say a 10% drop in sales taxes since the highway was moved, maybe 5% more since the layoffs."

Mehring frowned. He had hoped for bigger numbers, but he shrugged and turned to Boxboro's mayor. "Mary?"

"We're smaller than Milltown, about 1700 souls. The paper mill kept us going through the recession, but you can only sell so many cardboard boxes."

"What about tourism?" Mehring asked. "Isn't Abenaki Falls a big draw?"

"It has been, but five of the ten Boxboro people who were laid off were the permanent staff of the visitor center at the Falls. My cousin was its manager."

"What about the old Mont Rouge Hotel below the falls?" Mehring asked. "That used to be full to bursting on summer weekends."

"'Used to be' is right!" Mary exclaimed. Her mouth hardened to a straight line. "Glitzy motels along the new highway stole much of its trade, camp closures the rest. The Rouge is up for sale, has been for two years."

"Tax receipts?" Mehring asked.

Mary shook her head. "Don't know, but two gift shops downtown and one of two gas stations are gone." She grimaced. "We joke at council meetings about renaming the village 'Backwater.'"

"Better move fast," Wetherly growled, "or Purlin will beat you to it!"

"Mary," Mehring asked, "how much of Boxboro's decline can you blame on the park layoffs?" He hoped to ferret out a number he could use.

The mayor thought for a moment, then slammed her fist on the table. "Dammit, Bill, I can't say! Losing the park jobs was the last straw on a very sick camel. I know that, but I can't put numbers on it!"

Fearing that Mary's anger could be contagious, Mehring pushed back from the table and stood up. "Let's take ten," he said. "There's coffee, tea, and snacks in the jury room."

***

After the three mayors and Gus Schneider left the courtroom, Edie joined her father and Ron at the table. "Doesn't sound good, does it?" she said.

"Part and part," Henner replied. "The Milltown story is impressive, Purlin's not bad. Boxboro?" He frowned. "I'm hearing desperation in Mary and, to a lesser degree, Jim Wetherly. They may decide to take the state's offer of 25 temporary jobs and hope for the best."

"That would cut the legs off our case for a stay!" Ron exclaimed. Henner nodded.

Schneider returned to the courtroom a few minutes later, a cup of coffee in his hand, a scowl on his face. "*Verdammt!*" he growled. "Mehring is *so stark wie ein Stier* – strong like a bull he is! The other two they make pancakes!"

"They *waffle*, Opa," Edie said.

"Still, I see their point," Ron said. "Mary and Jim have to look out for their people. A stay won't help them if it means their jobs are gone for good."

"We need to think beyond the stay," Henner said.

"And beyond the lakes and camps!" a voice boomed from the back row of the gallery. Eustace Spinnaker had arrived late and slipped in when no one was looking. He stood up, tottered for a moment, then made his way down to the big table and sat down next to Henner. Ron noticed with amusement that his mustache was even, his face clean shaven. His sport shirt and slacks were pressed. Stylish Italian loafers had replaced his sandals.

"Henner," the lawyer said, extending his hand.

"Spinnaker," Eustace replied. "And the young lady?"

"My daughter, Edie. She's a park ranger, not here officially."

119

Spinnaker nodded at Edie and smiled. "Not official, but I have it from Mr. Tyler that she's a force of nature!" Edie looked down and blushed. So did Ron.

The old man turned to Schneider, whom he recognized from newspaper photos. "Tyler told me about you. He got mad when I said you're an old fool!" Anger flashed across Gus's face but vanished when Spinnaker added, "He was right. It takes a fool to wrestle with the powers." He grabbed Gus's hand and pumped it. "We should all be such fools!"

When the mayors returned to the courtroom a few minutes later, a tight-lipped Bill Mehring was in the lead. Seeing Spinnaker, he brightened. "Eustace! I'm so glad you could join us!" He introduced the other mayors and sat down. "I'm afraid Mr. Spinnaker has missed a lot," he said. "Should we summarize?"

Spinnaker shook his head. "No, no! I've heard enough to know that you've lost the forest. It's like the old days on the town board!"

Mehring blushed at the reminder of excruciating hours of talk that had led nowhere. "What do you mean about a forest?"

"You're thinking too small," Spinnaker replied, "focusing on the lakes and camps. They're just parts – small parts – of a bigger picture." He spread his arms wide in a gesture that reminded Ron of Charleton Heston playing Moses. "The Mill Run towns have been down many times. Iron. Textiles. The freeway. Every time, bold people – inspired fools – survived and rebuilt!"

The others were silent as Spinnaker, his forehead dripping, his hands trembling, paused to catch his breath. "If you see getting a few jobs back as winning," he said, "you'll get no more and may not get that!"

"Your point?" Jim Wetherly demanded, irritated by what sounded like -- and was -- a sermon.

Spinnaker ignored him. "Imagine what the valley could be like five, ten, 20 years from now! How would Milltown look, and Purlin, and…and…" He mopped his brow as "Boxboro" eluded him.

"Backwater?" Mary Strathmore asked. Her wry smile made everyone laugh.

"Boxboro!" Spinnaker boomed. "With a little money, the Abenaki camps could be rejuvenated and the visitor center at the Falls improved. The grand old hotel too."

"*Ja,*" Schneider grumbled, "*Mit Geld* – money – is all possible! Without…?"

Spinnaker ignored his objection. "Milltown's textile mills still stand and there are lots of iron workings in the park. A revival might include using a mill building as a museum for the iron and textile industries." He grinned. "There are even one or two abandoned estates on the ridge that could be converted to tourist hotels or condos.""

"Thinking of Spin Drift?" Ron asked playfully.

"No," Spinnaker said softly. "Spin Drift isn't abandoned, just neglected."

Bill Mehring had caught the old man's mood. "The Milltown opera house!" he exclaimed. "Tessie's!" Sunshine had pierced the gloom.

"*Ja, ja, ja!*" exclaimed Schneider. "But it is all *Kuchen* – cake – in the sky without money!"

"*Pie* in the sky, Opa!" Edie exclaimed. "And you have plenty of money!"

121

"Ach!" Schneider grunted. "A rich pig farmer is not Johann Rockefeller!"

Spinnaker smiled at him. "Don't worry, Gus. I have money, and I know how to get more!" He turned to Wetherly. "What about Purlin?"

The mayor scratched his head. "Well, we used to have a little artists' colony, and the town lies between two stretches of 15A that wind through pretty farmland." He thought for a moment, then added, "There's a cider mill, a sugar bush, and a great little fishing lake just a short drive into Mill Run Park on CR-3. We could upgrade our marina, maybe add a riverside restaurant, even a hotel."

"Come to think of it," Mary Strathmore said, "all of 15A, from New Westphal to North Fork, is beautiful. Why not ask the state to label it a scenic and historical byway, as Vermont did for old Route 7 through Manchester?"

Mehring looked at his watch and frowned. Spinnaker had galvanized the mayors, but it was almost nine and Ron's talking points lay untouched. "I guess we'll need to meet again to organize our appeal for a stay."

Henner shook his head vigorously. "With respect, Bill, time is critical: The bulldozers could move in at any moment. I propose that a subcommittee – you, Tyler, and I – compose a brief, e-mail it to all hands for comments, and get it to Judge Brandt as fast as possible."

The others nodded, but Schneider scowled, "Why Tyler?" He was irked to be left out of the writing after pushing so hard in the Senate.

Edie knew the answer: Her grandfather's damn the torpedoes approach hadn't worked in the past, and wasn't what was needed now.

She put a hand on his arm. "Because, Opa, as you've said yourself, Ron has camps *im Herz*. And he writes great English!"

The meeting adjourned with handshakes all around. After the other mayors left, Mehring took Ron aside. "The brief will be the easy part," he said. "We also need a position statement, something to rally public support for rehiring the park staff, re-opening the lakes, and saving the camps."

"An op-ed?" Ron asked.

"Exactly! If you'll write one, I'll see that it's published." Mehring grinned. "*The North Fork Herald's* executive editor is an old school friend."

Edie Henner had overheard their conversation. After Mehring left the courtroom, she approached Ron and gave him a hug. "Good meeting! Aren't you glad you went to see Spinnaker?"

"Very glad," Ron said. He tucked his recorder in his breast pocket, scooped up his unused talking points, turned off the courtroom lights, and followed Edie out the door. For a moment, they stood on the courthouse steps in silence, enjoying a rosy twilight that promised a blue sky the next morning.

"Now do you see where you fit in all this?" Edie asked as they walked down the steps and headed toward his Civic and her Jeep.

Ron nodded. For the first time since he and Jan left North Fork, he knew exactly where he fit.

***

Ron slept through the next morning's beautiful dawn, flattened by the tension of the previous evening. It was past eight when a shout from the kitchen roused him. "Deer!" Jan cried. "Two of them!"

Ron pulled on his bathrobe, stepped into his moccasins, and padded to the kitchen where Jan was staring out the window at a doe and her spotted fawn. "I'm surprised you didn't scare them away," he whispered. "If we go out, they'll bolt for sure."

As they watched, the fawn nosed around among the lilies. Some were budding, others starting to bloom. "My lilies!" Jan wailed. "Please eat something else!"

"Didn't the deer eat your father's lilies?" Ron asked.

She chuckled. "They wouldn't have dared. He was a hunter, with an eight point buck to prove it!"

After a few minutes of indecision, the doe, who had stayed out of Jan's garden, nudged her fawn to get him away from the lilies. He followed her into the woods behind the cabin.

Jan kept staring out the window for a moment. "They're so beautiful!" she exclaimed. "I almost wish we'd planted something they could eat!"

"Something tastier than marigolds?" He squeezed her hand. "You're softening. "I'll make a greenie of you yet!"

23. "Steps and Footprints"

As Bill Mehring predicted, writing a brief for Justice Brandt was easy. Working late one sultry evening, he, Ron, and Paul Henner put together a well-documented summary of the economic and social dislocations caused by the park layoffs. It showed that the state's plan to replace half of the lost jobs with part time, temporary positions would provide little relief for the valley towns. Even that would end once the camps were leveled.

Henner was sure Justice Brandt would see the wisdom in staying the state's hand for 90 days, or until the legislature returned from its long summer break. That would give Schneider, Synstrom, and other friendly legislators time to craft a bill to rehire all of the laid off workers, reopen the lakes, and spare the camps.

The lawyer e-mailed the brief to the mayors of Purlin and Boxboro. After he received their approval, he hand carried it to Brandt. By the third week in July, the stay was in place and the legislative campaign was under way.

***

On August 1, an essay appeared on the op-ed page of *The North Fork Herald:*

Steps and Footprints

In 2008, faced by a sharp, recession-driven drop in revenue, the state legislature passed a resolution to take a small step toward fiscal responsibility. It laid off 75 of Mill Run State Park's workers, closed five small, underused lakes in the western half of the park, and ordered that their few remaining group camps be razed "to discourage squatters and vandals and minimize a risk of forest fires."

Supported by the business community and environmentalists who saw a chance to return thousands of acres to wilderness, the bill passed quickly. Only removal of the camps remains unfinished today for want of workers to accomplish it.

Small steps can leave big footprints. Although the bill's sponsors foresaw only "some inconvenience for a few people" in communities adjacent to the park, the damage done went far beyond "inconvenience." A few unemployed workers left the area. Most, and some 200 dependents, joined the relief rolls when their unemployment insurance expired. That businesses were affected as well is indicated by sharp decreases in sales tax receipts in 2009 – 15% in Milltown alone -- and the shuttering of businesses there and in Purlin and Boxboro.

With the national economy recovering now, albeit slowly, the state now proposes to rehire a third of the laid off park workers on a temporary basis to finish closing the five lakes and raze their camp buildings.

Because these steps will give communities little immediate economic relief and none over time, the Mill Run Valley Association has requested and received a 90-day stay of the rehiring order. When the legislature reconvenes in September, MRVA's representatives will submit a bill to rehire *all* laid off workers, reopen the five small lakes, and spare their group camps pending an informed decision on what to do with them.

We of the MRVA applaud environmentalists' efforts to preserve the rapidly vanishing wilderness, but we believe sacrificing Mill Run Park's group camps would be misguided and, in fact, counterproductive. Since the CCC built the camps in the 1930's, they have brought thousands of boys and girls into day-to-day, nose-to-nose contact with nature. Many of these children – the writer included – have grown up to be advocates for conservation. *Camps have been a prime source of the informed citizens that our state and nation need to cope with growing threats to the environment.*

We believe the state should reopen two camps on Lake Abenaki, Sycamore and Y-for-All, that were still active when that lake was closed. We recommend that it go further. Other camps, for example Luther on Abenaki and three camps on Lake Menomini, closed so recently that they remain in very good condition. With little effort and at little cost, they could be restored to usefulness.

It is reasonable to ask whether the restored camps would be used. Many camps failed in the 1970's to '90's because of competition with sports and computer camps. Might an effort to revive group camping in Mill Run State Park come to nothing? We think not, for 2010 is not 1970. The popularity of conservation organizations like North Fork's Wild-4-Ever testifies to growing popular interest in saving the environment. We believe the market for group camps will grow with it.

Conservation's twin missions are *preservation* of our fragile planet and *wise use* of its resources. We cannot think of a wiser use for five small lakes than as training grounds for the next generation of environmental activists. If you share that view, please urge your assemblyman and senator to vote "Yes" for camps in September.

Ronald L. Tyler, Secretary

Mill Run Valley Association

***

Few people in North Fork recognized the essay's author, fewer his organization. Indeed, the byline startled Ron. He called Mehring that afternoon. "I'm what?" he asked. "Of what?"

Mehring laughed. "Before I passed your essay to the paper, I edited it slightly. The other mayors and I decided we need our own lobby. So far, the MRVA is just the three of us, Eustace Spinnaker, and a secretary. That's you. Gus Schneider, Paul Henner, and Senator Synstrom are *ex officio* members."

When Ron was quiet for a moment, Mehring said, "Right. I should have cleared the changes with you, but it was important to get our message out fast. I hope you're not offended."

Ron laughed. "Something funny?" Mehring asked.

"Yeah. I'd like to see my mother-in-law's face when she sees the op-ed. She's not yet gotten over my turning down Harvard. Now I'm a *secretary*?

Mehring chuckled. "I see your point. When we incorporate, we'll give you a more impressive title. How about 'Minister of Propaganda?'"

***

Reaction to Ron's op-ed came quickly in letters to *The Herald* and comments on Wild-4-Ever's Facebook page, where Mehring had posted a link to it. Most of the letters were hostile ("small-minded…" "… a cry for a treeless Earth!" "…typical liberal bleat.") Some attacked Ron ("Who elected him to question the legislature's decision?"). One letter called the MRVA "one more socialist pressure group." Ron and Mehring were not surprised that some of the Facebook comments were even more hostile.

Ron was pleased to find that a few correspondents praised his op-ed. Some comments came from people who had been hurt by the park layoffs, others from men and women who had camped in the park. "Bless you," one woman wrote, "for defending an institution that has meant so much to so many." Her eight-year-old granddaughter

128

had just started at Camp Sycamore when the state closed Lake Abenaki.

"None of this will mean much until Wild-4-Ever weighs in," Mehring told Ron. Its website reported on the op-ed on August 5. Its "Letters" section smoked thereafter, but as of mid-August, there was no official statement and no petition.

"Maybe the Baums are on vacation," Ron suggested. "Let's hope it's a long one!"

"Or they're holding their fire, saving their ammunition until the legislature returns from its two month break."

***

In mid-August, Ron received a letter from North Fork on English Department stationery. It was from Professor Moffett. "Well done, Ron!" it said. "Win, lose, or draw, you have found your voice and used it to good effect!"

Below Moffett's signature was a scrawled P.S. "Sam White sends his best. He's sorry you've passed up Harvard, but proud that he saw you through the Master's."

Ron resolved to write a long letter to White. The old man had led him up a garden path, but he had also taught him a lot about writing. More important, he had steered him through the darkest hours of his life. "Thank you!" would be kind and a way for him to write *Fin!* to his student days.

24. North Fork

On September 7, the first day of the legislature's fall term, Jan and Ron left Lake Menomini at six a.m., hoping to reach the capital before the opening session began. It seemed likely that the issue of park jobs would come up.

"I feel like a big cork in a small bottle!" Jan said as she wedged into the Civic's right front seat. "I want a Buick next!"

"After Thanksgiving, you won't need one!' Ron replied.

The tight fit aside, Jan was in good spirits as they drove down Route 15. In six months, through her library work, the knitting group, and conversations at the IGA and post office, she had made many friends in Milltown.

She had also come to think of Lake Menomini as home. "Sentinel trees!" she had cried on a late August morning when splashes of crimson and orange appeared on the green ridge across the lake. Fall was coming, bringing the promise of new life to replace the bump that made her ponderous and unsteady. "Thanksgiving can't come too soon for me!" she exclaimed as she struggled with her seat belt.

"For me too!" Ron said. Although his violent nightmares had disappeared after his meeting with Spinnaker, he had left their double bed for a single in the second bedroom "for logistical reasons."

Jan approved of Ron's effort to sway the legislature, but she was skeptical. "Doesn't lawmaking take lots of time?" she asked as they approached the capital. "Doesn't a bill have to go through subcommittees and committees and…."

"And joint committees to resolve differences between the Senate and Assembly versions? Yes, that's true in most cases."

"Most cases?"

"The bill to rehire the park workers is unusual," he explained. "Schneider has pushed it for two years, so it's not a cold start. And the legislature is under pressure to help people and communities that were slammed by the recession. It also helps that the economy is improving."

"If the case is so strong, why the hurry?"

"Aside from the fact that people in the valley are really hurting, there's the 90 day stay. If it expires and the legislature hires temporary workers, bulldozers will follow."

Jan was silent for a moment, thinking how painful it would be to leave their child's painted and curtained bedroom. "But what about the environmentalists?" she asked. "Won't they lobby against you?"

"Ah, the wild card!" Ron exclaimed. "We have to hope a fast move at the end of the summer will catch them off guard."

The bill still struck Jan as a long shot, but she nodded. "Call me when the session lets out." she said as she dropped Ron at the capital. "I'll be shopping downtown."

***

Like many such structures across the country, the state's capital, erected in 1912, is a miniature replica of the U.S. Capitol, with a central rotunda and wings for the Senate and Assembly. The Senate wing includes a modest chamber for the 21 senators (one per county). Because the architect anticipated that there would be times when the two houses would meet jointly, he made the Assembly chamber more than twice as big as the Senate's. It can hold 300 legislators, its gallery half that many visitors.

It is customary for the legislature to end its two month summer recess on Labor Day and reconvene in a joint session the next day. Because members trickle in for a week thereafter, the first meeting is largely ceremonial: An opening prayer by the Senate chaplain, recognition of new legislators, and "Talk Back Time," a chance for citizens to speak to their representatives.

Because no legislative business would be conducted until a week later, September 7, 2010 found most seats in the Assembly chamber empty. Among those present were Gus Schneider and Bert Synstrom and two assemblymen from the Mill Run valley communities. They and three people in the gallery -- Ron Tyler, Bill Mehring, and Paul Henner – were there because it was rumored that the Senate President, Jake Foster, had invited Armin Baum to speak.

At just 9:00, Foster, seated in the Speaker's chair, rose, gaveled the joint session to order and said, "Pastor Evans of First Presbyterian will give the invocation."

Ron switched on his recorder as Evans, a rotund man with a white fringe around his florid bald head, lumbered to the podium. "Dear Lord," he began in a time-worn baritone, "bless those who have gathered to do your work." After Evans rambled on for five minutes, Ron switched off his recorder to save its battery.

When the minister finally mopped his forehead and sat down, Foster asked the seven new legislators to stand as he read their names. Three people stood: two men who would replace recently deceased assemblymen and a woman who was a mid-term fill-in for a senator convicted of graft. Irritated that four new people were missing, Foster read the names, brusquely called for a round of applause, then turned to "Talk Back Time."

Ron switched his recorder on again and leaned forward, watching Armin Baum, who was seated in the front row of the chamber. To Ron's disappointment, Foster said, "Our first speaker is Kurt Grauman from East North Fork." Grauman identified himself as an undertaker who was concerned about overcrowding in the town's cemetery. He hoped the legislature "would authorize a small amount of double decking" to solve the problem.

The next speaker, a woman from Ron's home town, complained that aliens were interfering with her television and demanded that the legislature stop them. When she paused in mid rant, Foster said, gently, "The gravity of this situation requires a federal response." He promised to appeal to Washington.

Ron noticed that Baum was agitated during the second speech. He shook his head angrily when Foster announced the third speaker, Matt Doppeltag. The upstate farmer demanded that the county agent be fired because she had advised him to move his well from just below his piggery to a spot above it. "Damned well went dry!" he complained. Foster promised to speak to the Commissioner of Agriculture on his behalf.

"Remind me not to run for office!" Ron whispered.

After three more speakers whose complaints ranged from high taxes to flooded basements, Foster said, "We are grateful to those citizens who have shared their concerns with us. Thank you very much!" After a rustle of applause that died quickly, Foster said, "Our last speaker is my good friend, Armin Baum, President of Wild-4-Ever."

Applause greeted the tall, lean, gray-haired Baum as he walked to the Speaker's lectern. Ron replaced the tape in his recorder to be sure he caught every word of his speech.

"Friends," Baum began, "you may recall that in 2008, Wild-4-Ever supported the legislature's decision to cut staff at Mill Run State Park, close five small, underused lakes, and return half of the park to a

133

wild state." Ron saw many nodding heads. The few shakers included Gus, Bert Synstrom, and the upstate assemblymen. Jake Foster, one of the nodders, was beaming. "We did so," Baum continued, "because it was a rare – almost unique -- opportunity to recover wilderness rather than just save it."

A few people in the chamber applauded. Foster quieted them, but with a leer that made Ron's stomach churn. "That smug SOB!" he whispered to Mehring.

"Now, two years on," Baum continued, "an organization in Milltown has urged you, our legislators, to return the laid off park workers to full-time jobs, reopen the lakes, and spare the camps." A chorus of boos, mixed with a sprinkling of bravos made Baum pause while Foster gaveled for quiet.

"To judge by responses to a recent *Herald* article by the Mill Run Valley Association," Baum said, "a solid majority in Wild-4-Ever still supports the original decision and opposes MRVA's proposal." Applause rocked the chamber. Foster let it continue but silenced a few boos that outlasted it.

"Here we go!" Ron exclaimed, his stomach a knot. He noticed that Mehring was leaning forward, his mustache quivering, a vein in his forehead throbbing. Henner, his eyes closed, a faint smile on his lips, seemed to be at peace. "Is Paul asleep," Ron asked the mayor, "or does he know something that we don't?"

"Lawyers!" Mehring growled.

When the chamber was quiet again, Baum said, "It will surprise all of you, anger many, and please a few -- he glanced at Schneider and Synstrom -- to learn that I'm here to urge you to reverse the legislature's 2008 decision."

For a moment, everyone in the chamber was silent, too stunned to speak. Then "Traitor!" "Turncoat!" and expletives too raw to print echoed through the chamber, drowning out a handful of "Bravo's." The trio in the balcony stared at each other, open mouthed, then leaned forward as Foster gaveled for silence and Baum continued.

"Though well intended, the park layoffs hurt people in the Mill Run communities much more than they helped the state. That alone makes it imperative – *imperative* – to rehire the laid off workers." Ron thought nods now outnumbered head shakes as Baum's words sank in. He noticed that Jake Foster was staring at his lap.

"Now a word about camps," Baum said. "I believe the group camps in Mill Run Park should be preserved and, if possible, improved. The MRVA's recent essay reminds us that conservation involves both saving the wilderness and using its resources wisely. As its author, Mr. Tyler, put it, 'It is hard to think of a wiser use for five small lakes than as training grounds for the next generation of environmental activists.' I can only add, 'Amen!'"

Cheers and catcalls seemed closely balanced. Foster gaveled for silence, but it came slowly. Faced with the likelihood that Rev. Evans would give an even longer benediction, he decided to skip it. As the crowd noise lingered, he cried, "The joint session is adjourned!"

After the meeting, Gus Schneider and Bert Synstrom rushed to the stairs to meet Tyler, Mehring, and Henner. "*Fabelhaft* – fabulous!" Gus crowed, smacking Henner on the back. "We have a game!"

Henner shook his head. "No, Gus. All we know for sure is that Wild-4-Ever has a problem with its president. My guess is that Baum's hate mail will make Ron's look like Christmas cards!"

***

"I heard about the meeting on WRNF," Jan said when she picked Ron up in front of the capital. "Fantastic! And what a tribute to you!"

"I'm flat out exhausted!" Ron exclaimed. "Would you mind driving home?"

When the couple reached the ranger cabin, Ron noticed that his laptop was buzzing to announce incoming e-mail. He opened Hotmail to find just one short message: "Thank you!" It was signed, "Armin Baum, Camp Luther, 1980-84."

25. End Game

In the third week of September, Bert Synstrom presented a bill to the Senate that he, Schneider, and assemblymen from Purlin and Boxboro had written. It restored 75 full time positions for Mill Run Park, directed that five small lakes in the park be reopened, and recommended that group camps on those lakes be spared pending careful evaluation of their condition and prospects for future use.

Schneider and Synstrom expected the first part of the bill to pass easily, for data from the valley towns made it obvious that layoffs enacted during the downturn had cost the state far more than they had saved it.

The rest of the bill seemed viable too, for Armin Baum's statement to the joint session, reported in *The Herald*, had spiked the guns of those who wanted to make half of the park forever wild. Gus Schneider feared that the recommendation for evaluation of the camps would be "a red flag for the *verdammte* penny pinchers," but Synstrom reminded him that it required no new state funds. "It just puts removal of the camps on hold."

Hearings in the Senate and Assembly on September 23rd and 24th respectively, would prove Synstrom and Schneider half right. There would be little opposition to restoring the lost jobs, but the proposals to reopen the lakes and spare the camps would take heavy fire.

***

When members of Wild-4-Ever learned of Baum's change of heart, the group's Facebook page and website lit up. Most of the posts and letters played variations on one theme: Baum had sold out. The harshest comment came from Wild-4's vice president, Charley Mauch, who wrote on Facebook that Baum proposed to "throw away a unique chance to fight back against development." He added that "the president should be recalled, unless he steps down."

Baum didn't respond to the attacks. Long experience had taught him that those who agreed with him or wanted more discussion would weigh in more slowly. "And," he told his wife, Andrea, "Wild-4-Ever has no mechanism for recalling a president!"

He was right. By the time of the Senate hearing, almost as many members had written to support him as had opposed him. Baum noted with pleasure that several people cited their own camp experiences as the reason for their commitment to conservation. "It will be okay," he told Andrea, with almost perfect confidence.

***

When the Senate hearing on the Synstrom-Schneider bill began at nine on September 23rd, Tyler and Mehring were in the front row of a crowded gallery. Paul Henner was in court that day for a civil case. He planned to attend the Assembly hearing on the 24th.

To Ron's surprise, Edie Henner was absent too. "Where is she?" he asked Mehring.

"She's gone back to North Fork to finish her degree and start law school. Didn't she tell you?"

Ron shook his head and looked away as tears formed in the corners of his eyes. *Not even a goodbye!* he thought.

When he turned around to look at the men and women in the gallery, he saw that most were in their 20's and 30's, a few clearly on Social Security. From snatches of animated conversations – "forever wild," "outdoor education," "should step down," "our president"– he gathered that Wild-4-Ever was there in force, with both sides represented.

Ron recognized two of three men who were seated in the front row of the chamber, which was reserved for those who would make statements. One was Armin Baum, another – to Ron's surprise – Eustace Spinnaker. The third man, a few seats away from the others, was a head taller than both, with close-cropped, gray-flecked brown hair and square shoulders. Ron estimated that he was fortyish, a decade or two younger than Baum. "Who is that?" he asked Mehring.

Before the mayor could answer, a young woman seated behind them leaned forward and whispered, "Charley Mauch."

"Order!" Jake Foster commanded, and the buzz in the gallery ceased. "We're here to consider Senate Bill 2010-14, 'Staffing of Mill Run State Park.'" He looked at the assembled senators and, ignoring Gus Schneider, nodded in the direction of Bert Synstrom. "The bill's co-sponsor will stand for questions about it." Beaming at Mauch, he added. "We'll also hear from three concerned citizens."

Ignores Gus and leers at Mauch, Ron thought. *No bias here!*

Synstrom, in his late forties, wore a sport coat and tie appropriate to his status as a state senator. He took less than ten minutes and five viewgraphs to make the case for the bill. After he finished, there were several questions from the floor. They were soft pitches: "How reliable are your economic data?" ("Very!") "Aren't most of the camps bulldozer bait?" ("Two were still operating in 2007. Four others need only minor repairs.") "Won't the proposed 'evaluation' of the camps cost money?" ("Nothing beyond salaries and benefits for the rehired workers.")

Ron had begun to relax when, at a pause in the questioning, Jake Foster weighed in. "Mr. Synstrom, "the chairman asked, "would it be unfair to ask whether the proposed 'evaluation' anticipates repairing and reopening the camps?" Ron snapped to attention.

"A possibility, but....

139

Foster interrupted him. "There were twelve group camps in Mill Run Park in 1958. All but two were closed by 2008." Synstrom nodded. "Given that sorry history," Foster continued, "wouldn't it make more economic and environmental sense to just get the park out of group camping altogether?"

Synstrom mopped his brow and Gus Schneider squirmed in his seat. Ron imagined a balloon full of invective German over the old man's head.

"Interest in the environment...." Synstrom began.

Foster waded in again. "Yes, yes! Interest in global warming might – *might* – revive camping, if systematic warming is real." He leaned forward and glared in Schneider's direction. "This body must deal with *is* and *will be*, not *might*!"

Half of the gallery erupted in cheers, and there was some applause in the Senate chamber. Foster savored the moment, then dropped his gavel. "Now, let us hear what some interested citizens have to say. Mr. Mauch?"

Mauch, wearing a bush jacket and with the dark leather face of an outdoorsman, strode to the lectern. He swept his eyes over the audience, then the gallery. "Chairman Foster, senators, friends, "he said, "I come to you with a brief message from Wild-4-Ever. We supported the legislature's 2008 decision and urge the Senate and Assembly not to back away from it." He leaned forward and bellowed, "Let ours be the first state in America to recover wilderness, not just save it!"

The gallery erupted again. Clearly Wild-4-Ever was divided: Shouts of "Right on!" and "Tell 'em, Charley!" were interspersed with cries of "Save the workers!" and "Baum! Let's hear from Baum!" The girl behind Mehring stood up and yelled, "You don't speak for all of us, Mauch!"

140

Foster gaveled for quiet and, without a word, beckoned Baum to the podium. Having heard him speak at the joint session, Ron expected fire and brimstone from Wild-4-Ever's president. Instead, he spoke so softly that people in the gallery had to strain to hear him. He nodded to Mauch and said, "I think it was Emerson who conflated hobgoblins, consistency, and small minds. Obviously, consistency is not one of my hobgoblins!"

Chuckles in the chamber prompted Foster to use his gavel again, then Baum continued. "Two years ago, I believed recovering a patch of wilderness trumped saving a few jobs and some moldering camps. Now I realize that Wild-4-Ever's dream and mine cost too many too much." He looked out at the senators, then down at Mauch. "My right – well, left – turn has cost me friends. I hope they'll return."

Mauch blushed and looked down. Baum turned and looked at Jake Foster. "Can camps save the wilderness?" he asked. "Of course not, but campers who grow into concerned citizens can. I was one such. So, I think, was Charley." Mauch nodded but didn't look up.

Baum leaned forward and looked out at the senators, engaging eyes all over the chamber. Then he said, loudly, "I leave you with one message from many of us in Wild-4-Ever: Please reopen the lakes and spare the camps until wiser heads decide what to do with them."

This time, a few boos from the gallery were drowned out by a chant: "Ar-*min*! Ar-*min*! Ar-*min*!" By Ron's quick count, more than half of the senators clapped and a few yelled "Bravo!" This time, Foster was quick with the gavel. He scowled as the applause ignored him and died a slow, natural death.

It seemed for a moment that Foster had forgotten Eustace Spinnaker, but the old man stood up and shuffled toward the podium. "Mr....?" the chairman asked.

"Spinnaker!" the textile magnate said, in a loud, firm voice that startled Foster and brought the chamber to silence. Although Eustace had to grip the podium to steady his hands, his dark suit and regimental tie made it easy for Ron to imagine him dominating a board room.

"Friends," Spinnaker began, "Senator Synstrom and Mr. Baum have covered most of what I intended to say. Like them, I'm here to urge the legislature to save Mill Run Park's lakes and camps." Applause began in the gallery and spread to a few senators. Foster's attempt to squelch it failed.

Grateful for a pause to catch his breath, Spinnaker continued. "As you weigh the bill before you, I hope you'll consider another reason to pass it: History."

A puzzled murmur passed through the chamber and gallery. "Where's he going with this?" Ron asked Mehring.

"Just wait," the mayor replied.

Spinnaker continued. "The camps testify to the state's wisdom in creating Mill Run Park almost a century ago. They stand as monuments to the men of the CCC who left their homes and families to build them. They also honor generations of mothers and fathers – the *caretakers* -- who ran the camps and maintained them, often against odds."

Ron leaned forward and frowned as Spinnaker paused again. Would the old man have enough steam left to finish?

He would. "As much as the iron mines and smelters scattered through the mountains and the mill buildings along Mill Run, the camps and lakes are artifacts of a rich history. They should be preserved for future generations." He stopped, looked around the chamber, and said in a clear baritone that belied his six- plus decades, "Please, ladies and gentlemen, in your wisdom, pass this bill!"

This time, the applause was full-throated and Foster made no attempt to squelch it. Spinnaker smiled and bowed to the senators and gallery, then turned and shook Jake Foster's hand. "That sly old fox!" Ron exclaimed. "He's teeing up a pitch for funds to revive the Mill Run communities!"

Mehring laughed. "That's the 'forest' he was talking about at our meeting with the other mayors. A fox indeed!"

***

The Assembly hearing on Bill 2010-14 (re-numbered Bill 2010-17 for the lower house) was shorter than the Senate hearing, though the audience was larger. Tyler, Mehring, and Henner sat in the gallery with about two dozen young men and women, many in Wild-4-Ever tee shirts. Armin Baum and Charley Mauch were seated in the front row again, but Spinnaker was absent. "Yesterday pretty well wiped him out," Mehring said. "You can bet that members of the Assembly have heard what he said!"

After Assembly Speaker Kurtz brought the hearing to order, Assemblyman Fleet from Boxboro summarized the bill and defended it. Most of the questions directed to him were respectful, including one from Kurtz. Noting Ron's relief, Henner whispered, "Ephraim represents Belfield. He's younger and more moderate than Foster."

Although both Baum and Mauch were present, only Baum addressed the Assembly. Clearly, Wild-4-Ever's two leaders had reached détente. Most of Baum's speech reprised his previous address, but he began it with a disclaimer. "I am the president of Wild-4-Ever but no czar. Many of our members, and perhaps many of you, agree with me that Bill 2010-17 should pass, for both economic and environmental reasons. For those who don't, our vice president, Charley Mauch, is here to answer questions."

Ron gathered from audience reactions to Baum's speech and the civil nature of the few questions that the Assembly leaned toward approving the bill. Chatter in the gallery was almost entirely positive.

"Are there any more questions?" Kurtz asked. Getting no response, he gaveled the hearing to a close.

Tyler and Mehring sat back in their seats, exhausted by two tense days. Paul Henner, eyes closed, hands folded on his chest, seemed to be asleep.

"Cast iron nerves?" Ron asked.

"It's an old courtroom trick," Mehring whispered. "I think he picked it up from Charles Laughton in *Witness for the Prosecution!*" Henner didn't stir, but his subtle smile spoke for all three men.

26. "When You Come to a Fork...

On October 15, Governor Simkins signed a bill, "Staffing Mill Run State Park," that rehired the workers who had been laid off in 2008, directed that the five small lakes in the western half of the park be reopened, and recommended an evaluation of the group camps on those lakes. It was, almost word for word, the bill that Bert Synstrom and Gus Schneider had placed before the legislature in September. A competing bill to hire 25 temporary workers to raze the camps had failed in the Senate.

Schneider's reaction – *"Ausgezeichnet!* – excellent --" was echoed in e-mails, Facebook posts, and letters to the *North Fork Herald.* Ron received many personal notes, two of them from Professors White ("Proud of you...") and Moffett ("If you decide, in time, to return to academia...")

The message that touched Ron most came in a small invitation envelope with no return address. On deckled pink paper with a scrolled "E.H." on top was scribbled, "Congratulations, comrade!" followed by an "E" inscribed in a hand-drawn heart. Ron started to put it on the fireplace mantel with other cards and notes. Then, thinking better of it, he stuffed it in his pocket.

***

One morning, a week after the governor's decision was announced, Ron was at Camp Herzl, trying to fix a dripping pipe in its kitchen, when his cell phone buzzed. He pulled it out of his pocket and said, "Tyler here."

It was Will Orville. "First," he said, "I want to congratulate you and your co-conspirators on a great job!"

"Thank you, Mr. Orville, but..."

"Will, please!" the superintendent said. "I don't want to pull you away from anything important, but I'd like to see you in my office as soon as you have an hour or two to spare."

"Is tomorrow afternoon okay?" Ron asked.

"Fine! Let's say about two."

When Ron got back to the ranger cabin, he told Jan about Orville's call. "I suspect he's thinking about re-staffing the lakes. Maybe he'll need this building.'"

Jan frowned and looked away. She had been slow to appreciate the ranger cabin. Now, a month from her due date, the thought of a move made her shudder. Because a hug was no longer possible, Ron kissed her. "It's probably something else," he said. "The park's ad said 'up to a year'."

***

Driving across the park on CR-5 the next afternoon, Ron thought about their options if they had to give up the cabin. He had begun to look for teaching jobs, but mid-year openings were few and most of the available positions were temporary. Bill Mehring had told him about a sabbatical replacement in North Fork, but Jan vetoed that. "Too close to Mom," she said. "She'd want us to move in with her." On the other hand, a one year contract at a high school in Fairfield, CT, would put them very far from friends and family.

A longer shot was something Spinnaker had mentioned. He had decided to convert his family's mill into an historical museum and needed administrative help to get that project moving. He also hoped "someone" would write a history of the valley's mines and mills, and had made it clear which "someone" he had in mind. ("At times," Ron told Bill Mehring, "knowing how to write can make you a target!")

146

As Ron drove past the trailhead for Kettle Hole, Edie Henner came to mind. He still had her note in his pocket. *Best to just dump it*, he thought. *Old news!* But turning away wouldn't be that easy. When he pulled into the employee parking lot in front of park headquarters, a young woman in a Smokey Bear hat was climbing out of a Jeep four-by two spaces to his left. It took Ron a moment to notice that blond hair peeked out from under her hat and she was several inches shorter than Edie.

"Hello!" he said to the ranger as she passed the Honda.

"Hi!" she said, tipping her hat. "You work here?"

"Temporarily," Ron said. "I'm filling in on Lake Menomini." He thought to ask whether she knew Edie Henner but decided to let the opportunity pass. *One lady ranger*, he thought, *is enough!*

***

Orville was seated at his big mahogany desk. "Coffee?" he asked and offered Ron a chair across from him. "Black, as I remember it."

"Thanks," Ron said and sat down.

The superintendent got two cups of coffee and returned to his desk. "Ron," he said, "years ago, when there were a dozen group camps in the park, we had an assistant commissioner who oversaw their maintenance and helped develop park-wide activities: canoe regattas, dances at the Pavillion, and such." He paused to blow over his cup. "Like most of the camps, that position is long gone."

As Orville sipped his coffee, Ron thought, *Where is this going?* He was restless, recalling that the superintendent was given to long speeches.

But not this time. "If the job still existed, I'd offer it to you right now, without hesitation." Ron's jaw dropped. "I have it from reliable sources that you have camps in your blood and you're good with a hammer and saw."

Ron laughed. "I do light plumbing too! I was fixing a drip when you called. By any chance does your source have red hair?"

Orville chuckled. "One does. The other has a German accent!"

"But Mr. Orville, if the position doesn't exist…?"

"Will, please! One position we need to fill now is lake foreman on Menomini."

Ron slumped. *There goes our cabin!* Noticing his distress, Orville said, "I intend to hire someone with that title whose main responsibilities will be to oversee evaluation and restoration of the camps and find groups to use them."

Ron sat upright. "Me?"

"You, if you want the job. The pay and benefits will be good, and a four-by is included."

Ron thought for a moment. "I'm flattered, but I'm not sure how long I could stay. I really want to teach English."

"Understood. Two years would be great. By then the assistant super's slot may be needed and back. If teaching pulls you away before then, well, you've already done a lot for the park!"

"May I think about it for a few days?" Ron asked. "I'll need to fly it by my wife."

"Take your time," Orville said.

As Ron walked down the stone steps to the employee parking lot, he pictured it full and smiled at the thought that one of the four-bys lined up in front of headquarters might soon be his.

***

"Sounds great to me!" Bill Mehring said when Ron phoned to tell him about the park offer. "Now let me tell you something that may complicate your decision. I'm too busy with two day jobs to take on anything new, but I could use your help for two pet projects." He explained that he had run a popular evening writing class for many years, but had to give it up. "Night and day classes are just too much for old legs! Would you like to take on the night course, starting in January? For pay, of course!"

Before Ron could answer, Mehring said, "I'd also like to team teach English as a Second Language with you on Saturday mornings. There's not much money in it, but many Guatemalan farm workers up and down the valley really need help."

"I'm not certified to teach ESL," Ron protested.

"I am," Mehring said. "You can pick up what you need from me as we go along and get certified later. Let me know."

Ron put the phone down, walked to the kitchen window, and stared out. Jan's marigolds and lilies were gone, but an early frost had made the ridge across the lake a Persian carpet of red, gold, and orange.

"Trouble?" Jan asked.

Ron turned around and laughed. "The best kind: too many options!" He explained the choices that Mehring had offered. "Bill is close to retirement," he said. "I think he's grooming me to replace him."

149

"That's flattering!" Jan exclaimed.

"Yes, but the park job would keep a roof over us till he retires or I find something else. With a baby due soon...." As he always did when he wrestled with a problem, he was squeezing his forehead.

"Let me do that," Jan said, getting as close to him as her belly bump allowed and rubbing his temples. "Take the park job and teach writing at night. If that combination works, you can pick up ESL in the spring."

Ron sat down at the kitchen table, opened his laptop, and tapped out an e-mail response to Orville. As he did so, it occurred to him that Eustace Spinnaker might want a piece of him too. *I'll fit it in somehow!* he thought, then laughed.

"What's funny?"

"I was remembering what Yogi Berra said about choices: 'When you come to a fork in the road, take it!'"

"A philosopher?" Jan asked. She was too young and Midwestern to know about Berra.

"Sort of," Ron said, "and one hell of a catcher!"

27. Jennifer 2

By mid-November, Ron and Mitch Williams, the park's Chief Engineer, had completed a first pass from lake to lake, grading camps from 1 (ready for occupancy) to 5 (for demolition). Camps from categories 1 to 4 would receive closer scrutiny in the spring, and, in the best cases, repairs.

Ron had not been surprised to find that the three recently closed camps on Lake Abenaki were in almost perfect condition. "A little paint here and there, one or two rotten boards," he wrote about his old camp, Luther. Two of the three camps on Lake Menomini, Schoodic and Schuetzen, scored 2, in both cases because their docks needed much work. Herzl came in at 3 for an archaic septic system and plumbing problems that Ron had been unable to fix. Camp Lackawanna was beyond repair -- a 5 – but its level site and large parking area had possibilities. "Perhaps a small educational kiosk about the iron smelter south of the lake?" Ron scribbled in his notebook.

A dozen camps on three other small lakes – Huron, Mandan, and Ojibwa – had closed decades ago and were category 4's and 5's. Two of the 4's on Huron had a few serviceable buildings and good foundations for others, but they needed new septics and docks. Only one of three camps on Mandan made a 4. The others and three camps on Ojibwa were clear 5's, useful only as sources of lumber.

In their preliminary report at the end of the year, Ron and Williams would recommend that rehabilitation of the camps begin on Lakes Menomini and Abenaki. Huron and Mandan camps might be useful one day if group camping took off, but they recommended that Ojibwa be cleared of buildings and made "wild forever."

***

151

On Friday afternoon, November 19th, their day's work done, Ron dropped Williams at park headquarters, and turned west on CR-5. The camp survey was going well, and a half dozen adults had signed up for Ron's evening writing class.

The next hurdle for the Tylers would be the birth of their baby. Doc Brown still insisted that "the stork will deliver a new Tyler and a turkey on Thanksgiving," but Jan was miserable. She was comforted only slightly by the promise of a part time job at the library "when things settle down for you."

Jan's mother was on the phone almost constantly. "You should lie in near the hospital," she said, and, "It will be early. All Edwards babies come early!"

Jennifer proved to be right. As Ron drove past the trail head for Kettle Hole, his cell phone rang. The connection with Jan was poor, but he heard "baby" and "coming." That was enough. "On my way!" he exclaimed and pushed the four-by's accelerator to the floor.

Thirty six hours later, Jennifer Ann Tyler debuted at the medical center in New Westphal. She weighed eight pounds seven ounces (Or was it seven pounds eight? Ron could never keep it straight.) Although both Jan and the baby were fiddle-fit, they stayed in the hospital for two days "just to be sure."

Jan's mother flew up from North Fork and shared the yellow bedroom with her namesake for several days. When the time came to wedge into the old Honda for the trip south for Thanksgiving in Blackwater, Jan said, "You sit in front, Mom. It's crampy in the back." Jennifer buckled in, then turned, leaned over, and kissed Ron on the cheek.

Startled, Ron blushed and asked, "What's that for?"

"Just because," Jennifer said. Whether it was the joy of grandmotherhood or the flattery of a tiny namesake, it seemed that Jan's husband had redeemed himself.

If baby Jennifer arrived a few days early, Harry Emerson Edwards II (weight five pounds four ounces) set a family speed record. A striver like his grandfather and namesake, he beat his Christmas due date by a month and spent Thanksgiving at the university's Mid-State Medical Center.

A few days after Thanksgiving, Jan and her brother were planning a post-Christmas double christening. "We really hated missing Mom's traditional too much turkey dinner!" Albert said.

Jan laughed. "Not to worry! You can make up for it with a too much roast beef dinner after the christening!"

"And," Ron added, "you can be sure Mom froze a ton of turkey for you. Some things never change!"

28. Memorial Day

Memorial Day, 2011 dawned warm and bright, with a light breeze that animated dozens of flags in Milltown's Memorial Park and the red, white, and blue bunting on its bandstand. A large crowd, augmented by people from Purlin, Boxboro, and other valley communities, surrounded the town's battle monument and the dais where several distinguished speakers sat. They included Mehring, the other mayors, Senator Synstrom, and Father Simmons from St. Mark's Episcopal Church in Purlin.

Father Simmons would give the invocation. The guests would -- it was hoped -- speak only briefly, but Mehring had more to do. His duties included introducing the guests, performing the speaker's part in Aaron Copland's *A Lincoln Portrait,* and reading the names of the valley's honored dead. A trumpeter from the high school band would end the ceremony with "Taps."

***

"Hurry, we'll miss the opening!" Jan urged Ron, who was washing the breakfast dishes while she struggled to dress a squirmy baby Jennifer. It was 9:45. Father Simmons would speak at ten after a brief welcome by Mayor Mehring.

"Almost done," Ron said. Though he kept it to himself, he was in no hurry to hear Father Simmons, whose windy reputation preceded him. His meticulous dishwashing was tactical, and it proved to be unfortunate. The priest's invocation was briefer than usual. By the time the Tylers reached Milltown, the band had finished *The National Anthem* and Mehring was introducing the guests.

Because the park's lot was full and all spaces along Main and West Streets were taken, Ron and Jan had to leave the Civic behind the IGA and walk three blocks to the battle monument. "See!" Jan said testily when they found themselves on the edge of a large crowd, barely able to see the speakers far less hear them. She softened when Ron volunteered to hold the baby, who was showing a precocious dislike for public gatherings.

Bert Synstrom, whose part in the rehiring of park staff had made him a local hero, received an ovation that lasted longer than his remarks. However, Mayor Wetherly, running for a third term, strained patience with a long homily about community values. Ron judged from the brief, scattered applause that followed that Jim would face long odds in November.

As other onlookers departed, the Tylers wriggled forward. One family that left early consisted of a dark-skinned young man in coveralls and mud-spattered boots, a slender woman in a faded print dress, and a two-year-old boy. As they passed Ron on the way out, the man tipped his straw hat and said, "*Buenos dias* – good morning – Mr. Tyler!"

"Good morning, Jorge!" Ron replied. *Buenos dias!*"

"Who was that?" Jan asked after the couple left.

"One of our ESL students. Jorge's Bill's favorite. He supervises a small truck farm between here and Boxboro."

Ron kept pressing forward, eager to hear how Mehring would sound reading Lincoln's speeches. He wasn't disappointed. The old Shakespearean lacked the genes to sound like Paul Robeson or James Earl Jones, but his rich baritone made the silent crowd overlook that and the high school band's shortcomings. Even baby Jennifer was quiet, asleep against Ron's chest.

Mehring was near the end of *A Lincoln Portrait* when there was a disturbance on the other side of the park. A squawk – "*Grüss Gott!*" – and a flash of green identified its cause as a large parrot that was perched on a man's shoulder. Ron immediately recognized both the bird and the man, but his eyes were drawn to the tall young woman next to them. Even from twenty yards away, her cascade of auburn hair was unmistakable. It was Edie. *What's she doing here?* Ron wondered.

"...shall not perish from the Earth!" Silence prevailed for a moment after Mehring and the band finished their tribute to Lincoln. Then the crowd applauded as the mayor stepped off the dais and walked to the foot of the battle monument. "Ladies and gentlemen," he said, "let us now remember the men and women of our communities who gave their lives for our country."

"Let's go," Jan said. "Jennifer's getting restless."

"Not yet," Ron said. "Let's show some respect."

Jan suspected that more than respect made him want to linger. She had seen his reaction to the parrot's yelp and had noticed how his eyes kept drifting toward Edie. She shrugged, took the baby in her arms, and said nothing.

"Abbott, Charles, ranger, Korean War," Mehring began. "Bassett, James, marine, Gulf War I" caught Ron's attention because he recalled the surname from a rusty sign on Ridge Road. "Old mill family," he whispered to Jan. Some names of men and women who had fallen many decades ago drew little response from the crowd. Others from recent and ongoing conflicts brought sobs, embraces, or both.

"Campbell, Joseph....Cruz, Hector...." Ron watched Edie as Mehring finished the C's and began the D's. "Davis, Benjamin.... Daniels, Laurette...." When the mayor read, "Donovan, Carrie Ann, Airman First Class, Afghanistan," he saw her turn to her grandfather, shaking and sobbing. Gus wrapped his arms around her.

Ron felt his own eyes filling and looked away, hoping Jan wouldn't notice. Reaching for a handkerchief in his pants pocket, he was startled when another hand intercepted his and squeezed it.

The hand was Jan's.